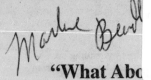

"What About Wyatt Couldn't Resist Asking. "You Didn't Feel Anything When We Were Together?"

"Look, you're experienced and worldly enough to take care of yourself," Grace said.

"You didn't answer my question." Wyatt studied her intently.

"I would have to be blind not to notice that you are a very good-looking man, Mr. Sawyer. But that's the end of it."

"So, I'm the only one in that room last night who felt any sparks between us?" he asked softly, moving closer to her. Her eyes widened.

"Yes, you were."

"Oh, I think not," Wyatt said, reaching out to unfasten the barrette that held her hair. "Still don't feel anything when I get close?"

"I don't think so."

"I think you do. Where's all that blunt honesty of yours now? Tell me if you feel anything when I do this." He wrapped his arms around her.

"Mr. Sawyer!"

"The hell with that," he whispered, and leaned down to cover her mouth with his own.

Dear Reader,

Get your new year off to a sizzling start by reading six passionate, powerful and provocative new love stories from Silhouette Desire!

Don't miss the exciting launch of DYNASTIES: THE BARONES, the new 12-book continuity series about feuding Italian-American families caught in a web of danger, deceit and desire. Meet Nicholas, the eldest son of Boston's powerful Barone clan, and Gail, the down-to-earth nanny who wins his heart, in *The Playboy & Plain Jane* (#1483) by *USA TODAY* bestselling author Leanne Banks.

In *Beckett's Convenient Bride* (#1484), the final story in Dixie Browning's BECKETT'S FORTUNE miniseries, a detective offers the protection of his home—and loses his heart— to a waitress whose own home is torched after she witnesses a murder. And in *The Sheikh's Bidding* (#1485) by Kristi Gold, an Arabian prince pays dearly to win back his ex-lover and their son.

Reader favorite Sara Orwig completes her STALLION PASS miniseries with *The Rancher, the Baby & the Nanny* (#1486), featuring a daredevil cowboy and the shy miss he hires to care for his baby niece. In *Quade: The Irresistible One* (#1487) by Bronwyn Jameson, sparks fly when two lawyers exchange more than arguments. And great news for all you fans of Harlequin Historicals author Charlene Sands—she's now writing contemporary romances, as well, and debuts in Desire with *The Heart of a Cowboy* (#1488), a reunion romance that puts an ex-rodeo star at close quarters on a ranch with the pregnant widow he's loved silently for years.

Ring in this new year with all six brand-new love stories from Silhouette Desire….

Enjoy!

Joan Marlow Golan

Joan Marlow Golan
Senior Editor, Silhouette Desire

Please address questions and book requests to:
Silhouette Reader Service
U.S.: 3010 Walden Ave., P.O. Box 1325, Buffalo, NY 14269
Canadian: P.O. Box 609, Fort Erie, Ont. L2A 5X3

The Rancher, the Baby & the Nanny

SARA ORWIG

Published by Silhouette Books
America's Publisher of Contemporary Romance

To Joan Marlow Golan and to Stephanie Maurer
with many thanks.

 SILHOUETTE BOOKS

ISBN 0-373-76486-3

THE RANCHER, THE BABY & THE NANNY

Visit Silhouette at www.eHarlequin.com

Printed in U.S.A.

SARA ORWIG

lives with her husband and children in Oklahoma. She has a patient husband who will take her on research trips anywhere, from big cities to old forts. She is an avid collector of Western history books. With a master's degree in English, Sara writes historical romance, mainstream fiction and contemporary romance. Books are beloved treasures that take Sara to magical worlds, and she loves both reading and writing them.

FOREWORD

Stallion Pass, Texas—so named according to the ancient legend in which an Apache warrior fell in love with a U.S. Cavalry captain's daughter. When the captain learned about their love, he intended to force her to wed a cavalry officer. The warrior and the maiden planned to run away and marry. The night the warrior came to get her, the cavalry killed him. His ghost became a white stallion, forever searching for the woman he loved. Heartbroken, the maiden ran away to a convent, where on moonlit nights she could see the white stallion running wild, but she didn't know it was the ghost of her warrior. The white stallion still roams the area and, according to legend, will bring love to the person who tames him. Not far from Stallion Pass, in Piedras and Lago counties, there is a wild white stallion, running across the land owned by three Texas bachelors, Gabriel Brant, Josh Kellogg and Wyatt Sawyer. Is the white stallion of legend about to bring love into their lives?

One

Stallion Pass

"**O**h, no!" Holding a baby in his arms, Wyatt Sawyer stood at the window of his Texas ranch home and watched a woman get out of her car. As she approached the house, his practiced gaze ran over her and he immediately scratched her off his list of possibilities for nanny. She looked like a child herself. Curly red hair was clipped behind her head with a few tendrils flying loose. Her lack of makeup and nondescript gray jumper and white blouse made her seem about sixteen.

"How many nannies will I have to interview for you?" he asked the sleeping baby and shifted her in his arms. He gazed at his five-month-old niece and warmth filled him.

"Megan, darlin', we'll find the right nanny. I'm going to take the best care of you I can." He held her up and kissed her forehead lightly, then returned his attention to the woman approaching the door.

Bright May sunshine splashed over her, revealing a fresh-scrubbed look that only added to her youthful appearance. Wyatt wished he could inquire about her age, because it was difficult to imagine she was a day over eighteen, tops. Wyatt's gaze ran over her again and dimly, he registered that she had long legs. He thought about two of the women he'd interviewed who were beauties. Both times, when they'd walked into the room, his heart had skipped a beat. Three minutes into the interview, he knew he could never leave Megan with either one of them.

He sighed. Why was it a monumental task to find good help? The pay he was offering was fabulous. But he knew the drawback—they'd have to live out on his ranch. Most women wouldn't accept a king's ransom to suffer such isolation. Those from ranching and farm backgrounds weren't any more interested than city women. Either that, or applicants were looking for a prospective husband, and Wyatt had no interest in matrimony.

The doorbell chimed, cutting into his thoughts, and he went to answer it. He swung open the door and stared down into wide, thickly lashed green eyes that stabbed through him with startling sharpness. For seconds they were locked in a silent stare, a strange experience for Wyatt. He blinked and studied her more closely. Faint freckles dotted her nose.

"Mr. Sawyer, I'm Grace Talmadge."

"Come in. Call me Wyatt," he said, feeling much older than his thirty-three years. How long would it take him to get rid of her? He had gotten the interviews down to twenty minutes per nanny, but this time he planned to give her ten. She couldn't possibly be over twenty-one.

"This is your little girl?" she asked.

"My niece, Megan. I'm her guardian."

Grace Talmadge looked at the sleeping baby in his arms. "She's a beautiful baby."

"Thanks, I think so. Come in," he repeated.

When Grace passed him, he caught the scent of lemons. Her soap? He closed the door and led the way down a wide hallway, his boot heels scraping the hardwood floor. He paused and motioned her ahead into the family room, following her.

She stood looking around as if she had never been in a room like it.

Wyatt glanced around the room, which he rarely gave much attention to. It was the one room in the house that had not been changed since his childhood, with its familiar paneling, mounted bobcat, heads of deer and antelope, all animals his father had killed. Also, shelves lined with books, bear rugs on the floor, the antique rifle over the mantel.

"You must be a hunter," she said, turning to frown at him.

"No, my father was the hunter. He liked to bring down wild, strong things," Wyatt said, knowing that after all these years he still couldn't keep the bitterness out of his voice. "Have a seat, please," he said, crossing the room to sit in a rocker. He adjusted the baby in his arms and rocked slightly.

Grace Talmadge sat across from him in the dark-blue wing chair, her legs crossed primly at the ankles and her hands folded in her lap.

"So Miss Talmadge, have you any experience as a nanny?"

"No, I haven't," she replied. "I'm a bookkeeper for a San Antonio sign company. I've had my job for five years. The owner has decided to retire and he's closing his business, so I need to find another job.''

Five years surprised him. Wyatt decided she must have gone to work straight out of high school. "Then why do you want to be a nanny? You realize it means living out here on my ranch?''

"Yes, I understood that from the ad.''

"If you've never been a nanny, what are your qualifications for this job? Have you been around children a lot?'' Wyatt leaned forward, about ready to escort her out of his house. She had no experience, which made him cross her off his list of possibles immediately.

"Actually, no, I haven't, but I think I can learn.'' Her voice was soft, soothing to listen to, but Wyatt's patience was frayed from too many interviews over the past few days.

He stood. "Thank you for driving out here. I know it's a long way, but I need someone with experience for this position.''

She stood, too, and faced him. "Have you had a lot of experience as a father?'' she asked, a faint smile revealing a dimple in her right cheek.

Startled, Wyatt focused more sharply on her. "No, I didn't have any choice in the matter, but I'm a blood—'' He bit off his words, realizing what he had been about to say. Being a blood relative was no guarantee of love or care.

"At least give me a little chance here, please,'' she said.

"Why do you want this job if you have no experience? You might hate being a nanny.''

She glanced at the baby in his arms. "Oh, no. I could never hate taking care of a little child.''

"Are you familiar with children?''

"I have some young cousins I've been around a little, but they live in Oregon, so I don't see them often."

He was beginning to lose patience, but he was worn out with interviews. "You're not here looking for a husband, are you? Because I'm not a marrying man."

She laughed, revealing white even teeth, and her green eyes sparkled. "No! Hardly. I didn't even know you when I applied for this. I have a friend in Stallion Pass, so I've heard a little about you. I suspect you and I do not have anything even remotely in common."

He agreed with her on that one. "Sorry, but some women I've interviewed do have marriage in mind, and they've been more than plainspoken about it. So if you don't know anything about babies and you aren't interested in the possibilities of matrimony, why are you willing to live in isolation with only me and my niece? Why do you want this job?"

"I've been putting myself through college. I want to pay off my college loans. I have my degree now, but I want a master's in accounting. If I have this job, I can save money, and when your little girl is in preschool, I can take classes while she's away."

"You're talking years from now. She's a baby."

"Time flies, and by then I'll have money saved. Right now, I'm paying back those loans."

"So when you get an accounting degree, I lose my nanny?"

She smiled at him as she shook her head. "No, not at all. It'll be something I'll have if I need it. Perhaps I can do a little accounting work while Megan is in school full-time. And if I don't do anything else with it, I already handle my own finances now and my family's, so I'll be better equipped to do that."

"Tell me about your family. Do they live in San Antonio?'' he asked, noticing that she had a rosy mouth with full, sensual lips. Making an effort, he tried to pay attention to what she was telling him.

"No. They're missionaries in Bolivia. I have two sisters—Pru, in Austin, who's a speech therapist and a volunteer reading teacher, and my oldest sister, Faith, who's a nurse and does volunteer work with elderly shut-ins.''

The warmth that came into her voice as she talked about her family gave Wyatt pause. He remembered his childhood friends, Josh Kellogg and Gabe Brant, who had loved their parents and siblings and been loved in return. He still remembered the shock of going to Gabe's home when he was a child and discovering that a family could be warm and loving.

"Here's their picture,'' she said, opening her purse and pulling out a photograph. She held it out to him.

"You carry a family photo around with you?'' he asked in surprise.

"Yes, I like looking at it.''

As he took the photograph, his fingers brushed her hand lightly, and he was aware of the contact. The picture showed a smiling couple, hands linked, and two brown-haired younger women, also smiling. Behind them were lush green mountains.

"These are your parents?'' he asked, studying the tall, dark-haired man and the slender, red-haired woman who looked too young to have three grown daughters.

"Yes. Tom and Rose Talmadge. They married young.''

"Fifteen?''

She smiled. "Hardly! They were eighteen. You're off just three years. They were childhood sweethearts. My grandfather on my dad's side, Jeremy, is a minister in Fort Worth.''

"Nice family," he said.

She pointed at the two younger women in the photo. "Those are my sisters. They went to see our parents last year, but I was still in my last semester at school and I couldn't go."

"So you come from a family of do-gooders, but you're going for an education in accounting and a good-paying job?"

"That's right. My family says I'm the practical one. Actually, I have a mind for figures and I like to make money. Money means very little to the rest of my family."

"Well, we have something in common there," he remarked dryly. "I like to make money, too. But I don't think your mind for figures will be a lot of help with a baby." He held out the picture. "Your parents look nice," he said.

"They're very nice," she said, taking the picture and replacing it in her purse. "I know you don't think much of me, but I come from a stable, hardworking family and I have good references. I think I can learn to take care of your baby."

Wyatt was intrigued by her. This soft-spoken, freckle-faced girl was getting to him. He knew why, though. Short of the tenuous bond he'd had with his older brother, Hank, he'd never known any kind of closeness in his family, and she was reminding him of his past in a way few people ever had. Clamping his lips together, he studied her, and she gazed back at him unwaveringly.

"Sit down and we'll talk," he said.

She sat down, crossing her ankles and looking as prim as before. She also looked as if she would run if he said boo, yet she had stood up to him with her question about his experience as a daddy. She'd nailed him on that one, all right. The first day it had taken him hours to learn to get a diaper on Megan the right way.

"The job means living out here on the ranch. It means living in this house with Megan and me," he reminded her.

She nodded. "Is there any reason that should worry me?"

"For one thing, there's the isolation."

"I don't mind that at all."

"For someone young, that's unusual. These are your prime years for finding a husband. Most women don't like isolation."

She smiled at him, her dimple showing and that twinkle returning to her eyes. "Getting a husband is not on my list of goals. I'll have your niece and I won't mind the isolation at all."

"You don't want to marry?" he asked.

"If it works out someday, but if it doesn't, that's fine, too. I have a busy life."

He didn't believe her for a minute, but he moved on to another subject. "I have a woman who is both cook and a housekeeper, and she lives on the ranch, so she'll be close at hand, but if you're nanny, you'll live here in the house."

She nodded as if it meant nothing to her.

"Since this will be your home during the week, I need to know if there's a boyfriend."

"No, there's no boyfriend. I've been working to put myself through school and I'm busy and I don't date."

"Being busy doesn't have a whole lot to do with dating."

She shrugged and he saw the dimple again. "All right. I've never found anyone who really interested me. I don't date."

"When did you graduate from high school?" he asked in a polite and legal way to discover her age.

She smiled. "I'm twenty-five. I graduated seven years ago."

Megan stirred in his arms, waking and beginning to cry.

"How's my girl?" Wyatt asked, patting her back as he stood. "Would you excuse me for a minute while I change her and get her bottle?"

"Certainly."

He left and Grace watched him go, a mixture of feelings seething inside her. Her best friend from college, Virginia Udall, had warned her at length about Wyatt, telling her of his dark past. How in high school he'd had to quit school and leave town in disgrace. She heard tales of his wildness, crazy pranks he'd done when he was growing up, the girls he'd seduced, drunken brawls in local bars. Virginia had an older sister who'd gone to high school with Wyatt. Grace had seen her high-school yearbook and Wyatt's freshman picture. She remembered staring at a picture of a boy who, in spite of wild hair that fell over his shoulders, was still the best-looking boy in the entire high school.

Of all the things she'd heard about Wyatt, the one that she could agree with completely was that he was the handsomest man she'd ever seen. When he'd opened the door, she'd been frozen for a minute, looking at thickly lashed, coffee-colored bedroom eyes, prominent cheekbones that gave him a slightly rugged look, a straight nose, a sensual mouth and firm jawline. The long locks were gone, but his black hair was still wavy and unruly, curling onto his forehead. The man was gorgeous. Small wonder he had a reputation with the ladies.

If was difficult to relate the stories she'd heard with

the caring uncle he seemed to be. She looked at the animal heads looming over her, the rifle above the mantel, the heavy leather furniture and the bear rugs. The room was masculine, lacking any feminine touch, yet she'd been told that part of the time, his brother and his wife had lived here. It was difficult to imagine a baby crawling over the bear rugs, and she wondered if the room had been that way since Wyatt's infancy. It was even more difficult to imagine Wyatt as an infant.

Was she walking into a wolf's den, as her friend had warned her? If she took this job, she would have to live here, alone with Wyatt Sawyer and a baby. Good looks couldn't mask the rogue he had been. For a moment, as she had approached the house, she'd been tempted to turn around and drive back to town. Then she'd considered the rumor in Stallion Pass that Wyatt couldn't find a nanny and was offering a huge salary. She had squared her shoulders and tried to ignore her qualms.

Wyatt strode back into the room, the baby tucked into the crook of his arm as he held a bottle for her. He sat in the rocker again, adjusting the baby and her bottle. Her tiny fingers moved over the bottle as she sucked. As he watched his niece, the loving expression on his face made Grace question the stories she had heard. The love he felt for the baby was obvious.

"Why don't you tell me a little about the job?" she suggested.

He raised his head and looked at her as if he'd forgotten her presence. Grace wondered if he still planned to send her packing. She knew he'd intended to earlier.

"You'd live here in this house and take care of Megan. I'd be around at night, but gone most of the day. The person I hire will be caring for my niece daily, so it's important that I have someone I can trust, someone who can give her tender, loving care and is competent with a baby.''

"I think I can do that.''

"It'll be an isolated life in a time when you might rather be with friends or out on a date," he said warningly.

She smiled at him. "Surely some time off comes with the job.''

"Yes, weekends. I'll take care of Megan then. Frankly, Miss Talmadge, you're young. I had someone who is more mature in mind, perhaps a grandmother with lots of experience handling babies. Someone who has no interest in dating. And that's another thing—if you do date someone, I don't want him out here at the ranch. No boyfriends allowed. I feel I need—''

Suddenly Megan shoved the bottle away and began crying lustily. Wyatt tried to feed her again and then he put her on his shoulder, patting her back and talking to her. When she screamed all the louder, he stood, jiggling her, talking to her and patting her as he walked back and forth.

"I don't know if she senses something has happened or if she's always been this way, but sometimes she's fussy. The pediatrician said she's in good health, though, maybe a bit colicky, or maybe she's just unhappy with the world.''

Grace set down her purse and stood, crossing to him. "Let me hold her awhile and see if a change in people helps.'' Grace reached up to take the baby from him. "You might get her more formula," she suggested.

"I don't think she'll take more," he said, looking at the almost empty bottle. "She doesn't usually finish her bottles.''

Grace smiled at him and took Megan from him, settling the baby against her shoulder, walking around and patting her back as Wyatt had done. She walked to a window and turned so Megan could see outside if she cared to look, and then she moved around the room. Megan continued to scream, and Grace held her closer and began singing softly to her. In minutes Megan grew quiet and Grace continued to walk and pat her.

Wyatt returned with a half-filled bottle, watching Grace as she moved around the room with his niece. Megan snuggled against Grace, who walked to the rocker and gently eased herself down. "Give me the bottle and I'll see if she wants more."

Grace shifted Megan in her arms and held the bottle for her. To Wyatt's surprise, Megan took it and began to suck while Grace rocked and sang to her.

With his hands on his hips, Wyatt studied the two of them. "For a woman who knows nothing about babies, you're doing a pretty good job," he said, still standing while he watched her with the baby. "Sometimes I can't get her quiet for an hour. Nothing suits her. I've taken her outside, walked her, sung to her, rocked her."

"Maybe she wants me for her nanny," Grace said sweetly, smiling at him, and he had to laugh. Grace's pulse jumped because his smile was seductive, irresistible, putting slight creases in his cheeks.

"I need to see some references before we go any further."

"I have them in my purse," she replied.

"Don't stop with Megan!" Wyatt said hastily, grateful for the baby's silence and apparent contentment.

"Tell me more about the job," Grace suggested.

"I'll be in and out. I have an office here and will have people out here sometimes when I'm working. Other times I'll be in Stallion Pass or in San Antonio. I'll have some trips to make. I don't know whether you know anything about my background or not..." He paused and looked at her questioningly.

"Very little," she replied.

"A brief family history so you'll know why I have Megan. My mother died when I was a child. My father raised me and my two brothers. I'm the youngest. Jake, my oldest brother, was killed when he was in high school. Last year my father died."

"I'm sorry," Grace said.

Wyatt stiffened. "We weren't close," he said. "Megan is my other brother's child. Hank and his wife, Olivia, were killed recently when their small plane crashed. They left wills appointing me as Megan's guardian."

"I'm glad she has you," Grace said, and he shot her a curious glance.

"Did you grow up in this part of the country?" he asked. No one who'd known him in the past would be pleased that Megan had become Wyatt's charge. Wyatt knew only too well the reputation he'd left behind.

"Yes. I've lived in San Antonio all my life."

"And you have a friend in Stallion Pass who's told you about me?"

"Yes, I do. Virginia Udall."

"I don't remember her." Wyatt wondered to what lengths Grace Talmadge would go to get the job. "You must really want this job, Miss Talmadge," he said, unable to keep the sharp cynicism out of his voice. "Most people in Stallion Pass aren't happy that I'm Megan's guardian. My deceased sister-in-law's family is threatening legal proceedings to take Megan from me."

Grace raised her head, and her green gaze met his with that unwavering look that held his attention totally. "I can easily see you love your niece and have her best interests at heart.''

''Well, you're in a minority. You also have no idea how I deal with her. Maybe I take her to bars with me. You don't know what I do.''

Grace smiled. ''You would never take this baby into a bar, and I bet you put her first in your life. Am I right?''

The woman was challenging him in her own quiet way. He realized his first judgment about her immaturity was inaccurate—something that rarely happened where women were concerned.

''You're right, I wouldn't take her into a bar and I already love her as if she were my own. For a novice, you're doing all right,'' he observed.

Grace glanced at Megan who had snuggled down on her shoulder, her brown eyes wide open. ''She's a beautiful baby.''

''Yes, she is,'' he said, a soft note entering his voice. ''Want me to take her?''

''I'm fine and she's happy. Go ahead and sit down.''

Wyatt was amused. Grace Talmadge sounded as if this was her house and he was the one being interviewed. As he sat, he arched a brow and tilted his head. ''If you were to take this job and move in, since we're both young, rumors will start. Are you prepared for that?''

She smiled at him as if he were a child with a ridiculous problem. ''I have no worries about rumors. My grandparents and my parents are in Bolivia, a little far away to hear rumors. My sisters and my friends know me, and I know myself. I don't care about anyone else or any silly rumors.''

''So you hadn't heard wild rumors about me before you came out here?''

''I have heard some things. If you had lived up to

them, I would have been gone by now, but you have been nothing but a gentleman.''

Wyatt had to bite his lip to keep from laughing. ''You tempt me to throw the gentlemanly facade to the winds, but I have Megan to think about, so the order of the day is to keep this impersonal and professional. One more reason I was in hopes of finding someone older. She would be more settled. There wouldn't be this temptation to flirt with you.''

''Oh, I don't think you'll have to worry about that at all. Men like you aren't tempted to flirt with women like me,'' she assured him.

''If I'd kept this interview professional, I'd skim right past that, but somehow we slid out of professional a little while ago. Men like me?''

''You're experienced and sophisticated. I imagine you like women who share your interests. I'm bookish, strait-laced and a lot of things that don't attract sophisticated men. Flirting will be no problem, not for me and not for you. Now, how soon did you want your nanny to start?''

''As soon as possible,'' he said, once again amused. In her own mild way, Grace was still taking charge, and she had neatly answered his question and taken them back into an impersonal interview.

''I want someone for the long term, not a continual turnover of nannies that will cause more upheaval in Megan's life,'' he said.

''You have no guarantees of a long-term employee with anyone you hire. An older woman could have something happen where she would have to quit just as easily as a younger one. I'm dependable. I told you, I brought references. My college grades are a 4.0 and my attendance in college and at work was and is excellent,''

Grace replied, patting Megan's back as she rocked steadily.

"Do you mind if I contact your current employer?"

"He doesn't know I'm applying for this, but it would be fine for you to call him. Along with my references, I'll give you his telephone number."

"Maybe we better get down to details," he said, leaning back and stretching out his long legs. "You would be on duty Monday through Friday, all the time, although when I'm here, I'll spend my evenings with Megan. I want a live-in nanny who will be a stand-in for the mother Megan lost. You'll live out here. Weekends are your own. No boyfriends on the ranch, no wild parties."

Her eyes sparkled with the last. "Am I to understand, then, that there will be no wild parties here?"

Again, she amused him. "I meant you, Miss Talmadge, but no, there won't be any, not by me or by my nanny."

"I find that satisfactory."

"You're trusting."

"Sometimes when you expect the best of people, they rise to the occasion. And if you don't, I'll be gone," she reminded him, still rocking Megan, who had stopped fussing and fallen quiet.

"Very well. I have some other interviews. Let me have your references." He crossed to her and Grace gazed up at him, her pulse skittering. "I'll take Megan now," he said.

Grace handed him the baby, and as she did, her hands brushed his and tingles raced through her. "She's sweet."

"You have her vote," he said lightly. As he took Megan, her face screwed up and she began to cry again. "Hey, baby. Megan, what's the matter?" He gave Grace a frustrated glance. "I don't know what makes her fussy."

"Maybe she's cutting teeth."

"She wasn't doing this with you." He walked around, patting Megan and talking to her. Grace, meanwhile, crossed the room and removed some papers from her purse.

"Here are my references," she said, placing them on the table. "Thank you for the interview. I can let myself out."

"Miss Talmadge."

As she turned to see what he wanted, Megan's wails became louder. "Just a minute. Shh, Megan," he crooned. Her screams increased, her small face becoming red.

Grace set down her purse and crossed the room to take the baby from him. He shot her a look, but then let her have Megan, who continued to scream for a moment, then quieted and snuggled against Grace.

"Maybe she does want you for her nanny," he remarked dryly. He had his hands on his hips, and more locks of his black hair had fallen onto his forehead. "You never asked about the salary."

"If you want me for a nanny and I want the job, I suppose we can work something agreeable out."

He told her what he planned to pay, and Grace stared at him in shock, because the sum was astronomical. "With a salary like that you should be able to get any nanny you want!"

"No. Women don't want the isolation unless it includes marriage, which it does not." He didn't add, but he knew that his unsavory reputation had turned many away. "The job means devoting your life to a baby."

"No, it doesn't. The weekends are free."

As she sat down to rock Megan, his phone rang.

"Excuse me, please," he said, striding out of the room. In minutes he was back, watching her rock his sleeping niece. "I'll take her now."

"And I must be going," Grace said, standing to hand the baby to him, too aware of their hands brushing. She picked up her purse. He followed her to the door and she paused, turning to face him. She held out her hand to shake his, conscious of his brief, warm clasp.

"Thank you for the interview. I'm very interested in the job," she said, looking at Wyatt holding Megan. He stood in the doorway, watching her as she climbed into her car and drove away.

A cloud of dust stirred up behind her car as she headed off. Grassland spread in all directions around her, and she could see cattle grazing in the distance. She would be isolated, but the job sounded good. With the pay that Wyatt offered, she could pay off her student loans, save for her advanced degree, get a newer car and still put some money away. She was astounded he hadn't hired someone already.

She wasn't afraid to live out on his ranch with the man, in spite of all she had heard about him. She said a little prayer that she got the job.

When a week had passed without her hearing anything from Wyatt Sawyer, Grace's hopes for the job dwindled. Three days later she picked up the phone at work to hear a deep, masculine voice.

"Miss Talmadge, this is Wyatt Sawyer. Have you got a moment to talk?"

"Yes, of course," she said calmly, while her heart jumped with hope.

"Your references gave you good recommendations. I was impressed. I did a background check."

"And?" she asked when he paused. She held her breath.

"You passed, as I'm sure you knew you would. So would you be interested in the job as our nanny?"

Two

"**H**e'll seduce you. You'll get pregnant and then you'll have to take care of your baby and his while he does what he wants and forgets all about you except as his nanny!"

Grace smiled at Virginia, who sat watching Grace as she packed.

"No, he won't. I'm not his type."

"You're female. That's his type."

Grace laughed. "You don't know what type of woman he likes. I think he's all grown up now and taking on responsibility."

"Wolves don't change their spots," Virginia grumbled, tossing her head and causing her long black hair to swirl across her shoulders.

"Wolves don't have spots," Grace replied.

"You know what I mean. Aren't you scared he'll creep into your bedroom some night and—"

"No, I'm not!"

"You know he had to leave town, and you've heard the rumors that when he was seventeen, he got a girl in his high-school class pregnant. She drowned soon after. A lot of people think he might have killed her."

"I thought you said that the drowning was officially ruled an accident."

"That doesn't mean it really was an accident. I've heard that he slept with every girl in his class."

Grace turned around, her hands loaded with folded clothing. "Some of those rumors are absurd, Virginia, if not impossible."

"No, they're not. I've heard that at least three kids in middle school and high school here are his children. He had to run away. He never finished high school."

"Just stop, Virginia, and listen to me. He is paying a fabulous sum, more than triple what I'm making. I'm losing my job because the business is closing. Do you realize I can pay off my loans and start achieving my goals? And think about how much I can save."

"It won't be worth your life. Money isn't everything," Virginia replied.

"Oh, don't be ridiculous! There is nowhere else I can earn a living like this with my background. The baby is sweet, and I'm not afraid of him. He and I will hardly see each other. I'm sure he's a busy man."

Virginia rolled her eyes. "You'll be a pushover for his charm. You've only ever dated two guys, Grace. You're Miss Innocent and he's Mr. Seduction, besides being the best-looking man in Texas."

"You finally got something right there. He is very good-looking."

"He's a gorgeous stud! I've seen him in town, and he's awesome!"

"I'll have to invite you out to meet him."

"You will? Promise!" Virginia wriggled with enthusiasm.

Grace laughed. "So it's all right for you to come out and meet him, but it's not all right for me to work for him?"

Virginia pursed her lips. "That's right. You'll be living under the same roof with him. I'll be visiting. You'll be his servant. I will have an independent status." She became solemn. "All joking aside, I'm not sure the money will be worth the heartbreak. I think he'll break your heart and grind up the little pieces."

"If he does, I'll have no one to blame but myself."

"Mark my words, if you aren't careful you're going to fall for him. No red-blooded woman could live under the same roof with that gorgeous hunk and resist him. According to rumors, no woman has ever been able to resist him."

"I'm not his type, I told you."

"That won't stop him from seducing you or breaking your heart."

"I'll be careful."

"Your parents don't know anything about your taking this job, do they?"

"Not yet, but I've written them and they'll think it's wonderful. They let their daughters lead their own lives."

"And your sisters are in San Antonio and don't know anything about Wyatt Sawyer. Are you going to tell them about your new boss?"

"Of course, but my view of him may be a tad different from your view of him. Now stop worrying."

Virginia stretched and slid off the bed. "Let me carry that suitcase to your car. I *will* worry about you, by the way. He's wild, Grace. All the Sawyer boys were and two of them are dead because of that wild streak. The first died in a car wreck—he was driving a hundred miles an hour, I've been told—and this other brother thought he could fly through a snowstorm when he was warned not to. And people've always said Wyatt Sawyer is wilder than his brothers.''

''I'm taking care of his baby, not him. So stop worrying about me.''

''I'm know I'm being a worrier, but there's just cause.''

''We'll see,'' Grace said, snapping shut the large suitcase.

Early Monday morning, Grace slowed at the front gate to the ranch, drove over a cattle guard and beneath a wrought-iron arch with the S Bar brand. White pipe fencing stretched for miles on either side, and the rolling land was dotted with oaks and cedars. On a far hill she saw Herefords grazing. Far in the distance she spotted a solitary white horse galloping across a field. The ranch was a beautiful place, and she looked forward to her new job. She tried to avoid thinking about Wyatt's reputation or Virginia's warnings. Following a hard-packed dirt road, she crossed a wide, wooden bridge, boards rattling beneath her tires.

She looked down at Cotton Creek, a thin, silvery stream of water. As she neared his house, she topped a hill and saw his sprawling two-story ranch house, more houses beyond the main one, a barn and corral and an assortment of buildings beyond the house and a four-car garage. As she recalled from her first visit, the whole place had a prosperous, well-kept appearance. When she finally reached the house, she saw a shiny black pickup parked on the drive at the side of the house, a large black motorcycle parked beyond it and a sleek, dark-green sports car parked on its other side. She frowned, hoping he didn't take the baby on the bike.

When she walked up to the door and pressed for the bell, her pulse raced. All morning she'd had butterflies in her stomach, but now her nervousness increased and the butterflies had turned into stampeding elephants. The door swung open, and she looked up into Wyatt Sawyer's dark eyes and tried not to stand there tongue-tied and starry-eyed. The man was sinfully handsome!

"I thought you might change your mind about the job."

"I'm looking forward to it," she said, too conscious of him, noticing the scent of his aftershave. He stood facing her with his hands on his narrow hips, and he wore faded jeans and a T-shirt. He gazed beyond her. "Why don't you drive around back? I can bring your things in for you."

As she turned and walked away, her back tingled. She glanced over her shoulder to see that he was still standing in the open doorway, watching her. Taking a deep breath, too aware now of herself, she hurried to her car. She was wearing her simple navy cotton skirt and a white cotton blouse, and she suspected he wasn't noticing her as a woman. She wondered if he was debating with himself the wisdom of having offered her the job. He had made it clear he'd intended to hire someone older and more experienced.

When she drove to the back, he came striding out of the house, radiating energy and strength. At the same time, she couldn't stop thinking about the ugly rumors about him when he was in high school. "Just keep your distance," she said quietly to herself.

Wondering what she had gotten herself into, she popped the trunk and got out of the car.

Wyatt put a bag under each arm and a bag in each hand. "Leave 'em and I'll get everything for you."

"I can take something," she said, picking up a bag. All of her suitcases had wheels, but he could doubtless see that and evidently didn't want to bother. She had to hurry to keep up with his long-legged stride.

"As soon as we put these in your room, I'll give you a tour of the house. This is a good time because Megan just fell asleep."

They entered a spacious kitchen that had a terrazzo floor, fine oak woodwork and pale-yellow tile countertops with a copper vent over the built-in stove. Grace's spirits lifted a notch as she surveyed her surroundings. An oval oak table stood in the adjoining breakfast room, which had a large bay window with a window seat that looked out on the rolling grounds. The kitchen was light and cheerful, far different from the gloomy family room where he'd interviewed her.

Grace followed Wyatt down a wide hallway, passing beautifully decorated rooms. She noticed her surroundings, but she was more keenly aware of the man striding in front of her, holding four of her heavy suitcases as if the things were empty.

She had brushed off her friend's warnings about Wyatt, but now that she was here with him, qualms and questions assailed her. Was she entering a wolf's den, walking into trouble that might cause upheaval in her placid life? Could she possibly keep from falling for him even if he barely noticed her and treated her as professionally as possible? Were the terrible rumors about him true?

He disappeared into a room and she followed, stepping

into a large bedroom with an appeal that took her breath. It was elegantly furnished in white and blue, and another grand view could be seen through wide windows.

"This is beautiful!" she exclaimed, looking around and comparing it to her tiny bedroom at home.

"Thanks," he replied casually. "There's an adjoining bath, too. Let me give you a tour, and then we'll get the rest of your things. I'll have to warn you right now, Megan has had a little cold. She's been fussy for several days."

"That's fine. I can deal with fussiness."

"I hope so," he said, studying her as if he could read her thoughts.

"You still sound doubtful, Mr. Sawyer—"

"Wyatt. Mind if I call you Grace?"

"Of course not. Why did you hire me if you have such doubts?"

He clamped his lips together, and she realized that either he hadn't found anyone else he thought would fit the job or no one else had wanted the job.

"You didn't have a choice, did you?"

"I just want you to let me know if you want out of this. A screaming baby can shred the patience of some people," Wyatt replied.

"She won't shred mine," Grace said, smiling. "She's a little baby. But I promise you I'll let you know if I want to quit. It's not Megan who worries me."

She wanted to bite her tongue and wished with all her heart she could take back those last words. His brows arched, and he focused on her with a look that made her want to be anywhere else but in his presence.

"Ah, all those stories you've heard about me, no doubt. The wild man of Stallion Pass. Lago County's bad boy. Is that what worries you?"

She decided this is what people referred to when they talked about being between a rock and a hard place. If she told him what was really worrying her, that she was attracted to her handsome employer, that would be dreadful. But it was equally appalling to tell him that his reputation worried her. Why had she blurted out what she had?

"In caring for Megan, I may have a difficult time pleasing you," she said.

One brow arched higher, and he gave her an intense look. "I don't think that's what you were referring to at all."

"Maybe not," she said, feeling her face grow warm, "but I think we should leave it at that."

He shrugged and turned away. "Come on, I'll show you the house." He crossed the room to open a door. "Your room adjoins the nursery. I hope that's all right."

"Of course." She glanced into a pink room with a circus motif and almost as large as her bedroom. She could see the baby sleeping in her crib, a mobile of Disney characters hanging above one end. Wyatt closed the door and Grace realized how close to him she stood. She stepped back quickly and he moved past her. "We could go through the nursery, but we'll go around it, instead. My room connects to it on the other side."

This was less-than-thrilling news. Grace frowned and tried to push aside her worries.

As she walked down the hall with him, he motioned her into a room that ran the length of one end of the house. His king-size bed was covered in a deep-green comforter. Surprisingly, shelves with books lined one wall. "That's a lot of books. Do you do much reading?"

"Nope. This house is much like Hank and Olivia left

it, and the books were theirs. I'm slowly going through things and changing what I want to change."

A broad stone fireplace was at another end of the room with Navajo rugs on the highly polished hardwood floor. A bowl of chocolates sat on the corner of a desk. Wyatt picked the bowl up and offered her one. When she declined with a shake of her head, he took a dark chocolate and set the bowl back on the desk.

"You have a beautiful home."

"Thanks, but I can't take credit. My sister-in-law did all the decorating, and they stayed out here some, but not often. She preferred to live in San Antonio. The only room she didn't do over was the family room, and I'm having it done soon. I'm not living with *that* reminder of my childhood."

He sounded so bitter that Grace glanced at him sharply. "Your childhood wasn't happy?"

"Hardly."

"I'm sorry. I was fortunate there."

"It was a long time ago, and you're lucky."

"I can settle in while Megan is sleeping," she said, reminding herself to keep things impersonal. "You show me what you want me to do."

He nodded and gave her a tour of the house, part of which had been built by his great-great-grandfather; the rest had been added through the years. In the paneled room that was his office, he motioned to a stack of letters on the edge of an otherwise clean desk. "Those are applications for the nanny position. I could have kept on interviewing for the rest of the month."

Amazed, she turned to him. "If you have so many possibilities, why did you hire me? Were you in a rush for some reason?"

"Nope." He rested his hands on his hips again. "I've

interviewed too many women to count and still had all those applications. I glanced through them. I'm the new guy in the neighborhood, and a lot of single women want a date. It's not that I'm so adorable or charming. I'm just new here.''

"You're not new at all. You grew up here," she protested.

"I've been away a long time, and some people don't know me or anything about me.''

"And how did you know that I didn't apply because I wanted to date you?''

Amusement twinkled in his eyes. "You didn't send me a cute, flirty résumé. You sounded quite earnest about the job. And when I asked if you had marriage in mind, you said no.'' His brows arched. "Did I assume wrong?''

"Oh, my, no!'' she replied, and saw the corners of his mouth lift in a faint smile. "I'm sorry,'' she added quickly. "It's just that this is a job—dating has no part in it.''

"I'm teasing. Forget it. You told me you weren't interested.'' He picked up the letters and walked around the desk to toss them in the trash.

"How do you know that there wasn't that one perfect, older, mature, grandmotherly type in those letters?''

"I read through them. I've had so many interviews, I don't think I can stand one more.''

"So I was sort of chosen by default.''

"No, not really. That day you were out here, you had a connection with Megan. That was important.''

The dining room was another large room with a fireplace. As they walked into the room, she heard a baby's wail through the intercom.

"Megan is awake. You can come with me to get her.''

Grace hurried with him, and at the nursery door, he

stepped aside to let her enter first, but then he moved past her to pick up the crying baby. As he bent over the crib, his T-shirt clung tightly, revealing the ripple of muscles. Grace watched the flex of muscles in his back and arms. His broad shoulders tapered to a slim waist and narrow hips. How was she going to work with this man daily and keep everything impersonal? Just watching him, she felt flushed and warm.

"Have you ever changed a diaper before?" he asked.

"Oh, yes. After my interview with you, I baby-sat a friend's three-month-old baby several times so I could practice."

"Good," he said, holding Megan on his shoulder and patting her. She quieted and he moved to a changing table, changing her diaper swiftly and then picking her up again. "I think I better get a bottle first and then I'll show you where all her things are and go over her schedule."

"Let me give her the bottle so she'll begin to get accustomed to me," Grace said. Wyatt nodded and handed Megan to her.

"Hi, Megan," Grace said softly, holding the baby up on her shoulder and patting her. From that moment, for the rest of the day, Grace was busy with the baby and learning about the house and schedules and what Wyatt expected.

"I'll take care of her at night," Wyatt said that evening when he gave Megan a bottle. "The only time you have to take over duties after bedtime is when I'm away. Whenever I'm around in the evening, I'll take care of her."

"I can help. After all, I'll be here, anyway," Grace said.

Megan was fussing and Grace and Wyatt took turns

walking her, the only thing that seemed to quiet her. At one point Wyatt told Grace to eat supper. Then she looked after Megan so he could eat.

While Wyatt got Megan to sleep, Grace went to her room to unpack. She could hear him in the nursery, talking and singing softly to Megan, and later, the creak of the rocking chair.

Grace put her clothes in a large chest of drawers, looking again at the beautiful room where she would live. Too clearly, though, she could remember Wyatt standing in it, watching her curiously with his brows arched. There were moments when he seemed to focus his full attention on her, and those moments made her pulse race.

It was difficult to reconcile the man who was rocking and singing to a tiny baby in the next room with the person who ran out on a young woman he got pregnant when they were in high school. If anyone seemed the perfect, totally caring father to a baby, it was Wyatt Sawyer. Perhaps the years had changed him.

It was after midnight and the house was quiet when she showered and dressed in her short blue nightgown. She brushed out her hair, climbed into bed and fell asleep.

She had no idea what time it was when she stirred at the sound of Megan crying. She remembered Wyatt saying he would get up in the night with Megan, so she tried to go back to sleep, but the baby continued crying until finally Grace threw back the sheet and got up. She pulled on her blue cotton robe and hurried to the nursery to check on the baby. She noticed the open door to Wyatt's room. How could he sleep through Megan's crying?

Avoiding glancing in the direction of Wyatt's bed, Grace rushed to close his door. While Megan cried, Grace switched on a small table lamp.

"Are you hungry, sweetie?" she asked softly, picking the baby up and walking her, trying to quiet her. She remembered where Wyatt kept formula and bottles and turned to carry Grace to the kitchen.

Just then the door to Wyatt's room flew open. He started into the room, saw Grace with Megan and froze.

Three

***

Wyatt had heard Megan crying and then rolled out of bed, yanking on his briefs. For more than two weeks he'd been up most nights and he was groggy. He swung open the nursery door, started into the room and stopped abruptly. A light was on, and Grace was holding Megan in her arms.

Neither of them moved. He stared into her startled green eyes. Whatever surprise she felt, he was certain his was greater.

Coming out of a deep sleep, he had temporarily forgotten her presence. Now he faced a woman who looked entirely different from the person he'd interviewed and hired. Her riot of red hair was down, framing her face and tumbling over her shoulders. She held Megan gently in her arms. She looked disheveled, earthy, appealing. He felt something twist deep inside. She wore a cotton robe that had been pushed open by the baby resting against her. Beneath the robe she wore a skimpy, blue nightie that revealed lush breasts and long, shapely legs. His gaze snapped up to catch her looking at him, and her cheeks were pink. He realized he was only in his briefs.

"Sorry. I forgot," he said in a husky voice.

She turned swiftly, trying to close her robe. "I'll get her bottle. I heard her crying and didn't think you would wake. I can take care of her."

With Megan in her arms, Grace made her escape from the room. Wyatt still stood there in shock. He'd hired a beautiful woman. Standing there in the soft light, she'd looked gorgeous. He rubbed his eyes, wishing he could erase the image and go back to seeing her as plain and his nanny and nothing more. But there was no erasing the image that taunted him now.

"Hell," he muttered, and returned to his room to yank on his jeans. He raked his fingers through his hair and headed for the kitchen. "I knew I should have hired someone a thousand years old. A grandmother with wrinkles and experience."

Grace was trying to mix formula with one hand, jiggling Megan who continued to cry with the other arm. Grace's back was to the doorway, but she turned to look at him when he came in. She had her robe pulled together, but he still could imagine the delectable body underneath the cotton.

"I haven't changed her yet," Grace said. "If you'll do that, I'll have her bottle ready when you're done and I can give it to her."

"Sure," he said, without thinking about what he was answering. Crossing the room, he took the baby from her. The moment he was close enough to reach for Megan, Grace looked up at him. Her eyes seemed to envelop him and pull him into depths that were filled with mystery.

He could smell a fresh, soapy scent and that riotous red hair was an invitation for a man to bury his fingers in its softness. Her skin was rosy, perfect even with the smattering of freckles on her nose.

He dropped his gaze to her mouth, which was full and tempting. What would happen if he leaned down and kissed her? Even worse, as he stared at her unable to move, he could feel the tension snap in the air between them. Sparks sizzled and danced. He didn't want any complications in his life right now, and he sure as hell didn't want to find his nanny so physically appealing.

Tearing his eyes from her, he took the baby, too aware of his hands touching Grace as he did so. Megan had her small fist wound around the collar of Grace's robe, pulling it open and for a brief instant, Wyatt looked at soft curves and flawless, rosy skin. His mouth went dry and he moved automatically, taking the baby and turning away.

"Come on, Megan. I'll get you changed and fed," he said, hurrying out of the room. His voice was husky and raw.

When in his life had he run from a good-looking woman? He was in a sweat, too aware of Grace. She hadn't been with him twenty-four hours. He swore under his breath and looked at Megan, who was still bawling. "Sorry about my language, darlin'," he said even though he knew she neither heard nor understood him.

He changed her diaper swiftly and scooped her up, intending to carry her back to the kitchen, but when he turned, Grace stood in the nursery doorway. She had her robe belted and buttoned, but the last button stopped above her knees. She carried the bottle and came toward him. He took a deep breath, noticing that with each step, her robe flipped open, revealing brief, tantalizing flashes of her legs. He couldn't remember what she'd worn during the day or for her interview, but both times her legs had been covered almost to her ankles.

"Let me hold her. I'll give her her bottle," Grace said. "I'm not sleepy now."

Neither was he, although for the past few nights he'd thought he would have given away the ranch just to have someone watch Megan so he could sleep.

Wordlessly, he handed over his niece, once again acutely aware of touching Grace, of standing close to her, knowing he was going through some firsts in his life. When had he ever been around a good-looking woman and not flirted with her? Never until now.

"I can feed her if you want to go back to bed," he offered, unable to keep the gruff note out of his voice, fighting the image of Grace in bed.

"I don't mind," she said. "I've been getting plenty of sleep lately, and I'll bet you haven't."

"No, I haven't. Thanks," he said abruptly, then turned and went back to his room. He closed the door, crossed the room and punched his pillow hard. "Hellfire!" he whispered.

Grace's soft voice singing a lullaby came through the door, and he glared at the door with his fists on his hips. Megan was quiet, and he could hear Grace singing, hear the creak of the rocker and all too well, could picture Grace holding his niece in her arms.

What was he going to do? He raked his fingers through his hair.

Eating a piece of chocolate, he paced the room and stopped to stare out the darkened window. Yard lights lit up the fenced area around his house. Beyond that, the trees created inky shadows beneath a quarter moon. It still surprised him that all this belonged to him now. Everything had happened so fast after Hank and Olivia's fatal accident. He needed to get back to California to see about his commercial real-estate business there. He was signed up for a bull-riding event in an upcoming rodeo in Sacramento next month. He had one in San Antonio, too, the last week of July. He could either withdraw from the California rodeo, or—what he'd planned—take Megan and her nanny with him.

Scratch that plan. He raked his fingers through his hair. He glanced over his shoulder at the closed door and could still hear Grace singing softly.

He could fire her tomorrow. Just tell her it wasn't going to work out, pay her a huge lump sum and send her packing. He could find a day care for Megan—if Stallion Pass had such a thing. He shook his head. Megan had lost her parents, and he didn't want to cause more upheaval in her life. He wanted her cared for at home with someone he could rely on.

Someone mature, kind and loving who had already raised children and loved them. Not a little redheaded sorceress who had a body that was sinfully tempting and a sharp mind.

He had never been in a dilemma like this. Attractive, sexy women had always been part of his life, but not as employees. He groaned and raked his fingers through his hair, pacing the room.

Through the years, he and Hank had kept in touch, and as he'd promised, Hank had always kept Wyatt's whereabouts a secret, because Wyatt had wanted to cut all ties to Stallion Pass and his father. No one here had known anything about him except Hank. Hank hadn't even told Olivia. Wyatt remembered when Hank had called him about his will. Hank and Olivia were making wills, and he asked Wyatt if he would be Megan's guardian if something happened to both of them. Olivia didn't want her parents to be Megan's guardians, because they had little interest in their granddaughter, and Olivia considered them too old to be bringing up a baby.

Wyatt had agreed, thinking the chances of Hank and Olivia dying at the same time were very slight. But the impossible had happened.

Now here he was with little Megan and in dire need of another nanny. He didn't like the thought of going through more interviews. He paced the room and debated what to do, until he noticed the time. Grace had stopped singing and Megan had stopped crying, but he could still hear the creak of the rocking chair.

He might as well relieve Grace and let her sleep because he wasn't going to, anyway.

"Dammit," he whispered, still fighting to keep images of Grace out of his head, trying to ignore the instant desire that had ignited when he'd been with her.

He was tempted to get on his motorcycle and ride through the night. He sighed. This was one time he couldn't escape. He had a baby to care for now.

He opened the door to the nursery quietly. A small lamp was still lit. It had a pink-striped shade and circus animals around its wooden base and shed a soft halo of light, leaving corners of the room in shadows.

Grace rocked, her robe open over her knees, her head tilted against the chair. Megan was sprawled against her, her little arm around Grace's neck. With her curls framing her face, her head back to reveal the graceful curve of her pale, slender throat, Grace looked beautiful. She was both tempting and maternal with the baby in her arms. Her eyes were closed, but she rocked steadily, so he knew she had to be awake.

Megan's eyes were also closed, but Wyatt knew how easily those brown eyes could open.

He moved closer. His pulse jumped, his mouth had gone dry and he was once again on fire. He paused before he got too close.

"Grace," he whispered. "Why don't you let me take her now and you go to bed?"

Her eyes came open slowly and met his, and the effect was like a blow to his middle. He wanted to lean down and kiss her. Sparks ignited and sizzled, and he couldn't imagine that she didn't feel something.

"I'm fine. I really don't mind. I thought you'd be asleep," she said, sounding sleepy.

"I can't sleep," he snapped. "If I'm going to be up, anyway, I might as well take her."

Grace looked at the baby in her arms. Megan's eyes had come open and she stared solemnly at Grace. "She's not asleep."

"I wish I had her energy. I've always thought I needed little sleep, but she can outlast me," he said, wishing Grace would hand over Megan and get the hell out of the room. He was going to have to fire Grace. He couldn't go through this day after day and night after night.

"I hate to disturb her," Grace said. "She's awake but barely, and she's content. I'll rock her. You go to bed. If you can't sleep, go drink some hot chocolate."

He wanted to gnash his teeth. "I don't need hot chocolate," he said abruptly, and turned to leave the room. At the door he paused. "I'm going for a ride on my bike. You can reset the alarm if you want, but Napoleon is in the yard and he's a good watchdog. We've got lights everywhere around the house, too."

"We'll be fine. I'll reset the alarm if I put her down and go to bed."

He did not want to think about Grace going to bed. Under his roof, in his house, only a small room away from his. Why the hell had he hired her?

He closed the door quietly, yanked on a T-shirt and boots and pocketed his keys. He walked through the house, turned off the alarm, stepped outside and locked the door behind him.

A shaggy dog came bounding up, and Wyatt scratched his ears. "Napoleon, you watch the house, y'hear? I'll be back."

The dog trotted at his heels until Wyatt stepped through the back gate. He closed and latched the gate and looked at the big dog, a cross between a collie and a German shepherd. "You're on guard now."

The dog wagged his tail and sat. Wyatt strode across the drive into the open garage to get his bike. In minutes he roared away, racing through the night and heading up the road.

Within two hours he was back, sleepy, grumpy and as on fire as he'd been when he left. Never in his life had a woman tied him in knots like this. And she wasn't doing anything except just being there.

"Get a grip," he told himself, striding toward the house and praying Megan and Grace were asleep. He would take a cold shower, have a slug of whiskey and hope he could get a few hours' sleep. He was too aware that the sun would be coming over the horizon all too soon, and he hadn't had a good night's sleep since he had inherited Megan.

He would fire Grace. For his peace of mind, she had to go. Every time he made that decision, he thought about being in the lurch again for a nanny and all the interviews he would have to do.

Seduce her, a treacherous part of his mind told him. That way he could get some peace of mind, have a woman in his life, in his house, and still have a nanny.

No. That wouldn't work. He didn't want some starry-eyed virgin who wouldn't give Megan her full attention. Also, Wyatt knew that he had left town with a terrible cloud over his head. At seventeen he hadn't given a damn, but now he had Megan to think about, and for her sake, he needed to be a respectable, settled, upstanding citizen. The thought made him shake his head.

Since when had anyone in Stallion Pass or the next three counties thought of him as respectable? But they were going to. He never wanted to hurt Megan in any manner and he'd toss aside his wild ways for her sake.

So it came back to getting rid of Grace. He sighed. He could fish those applications for nanny out of the trash before Mrs. Perkins, the housekeeper, got them.

He peeked in on Megan and was relieved to see she was asleep and Grace was nowhere in sight. He tiptoed farther into the nursery to look at the baby, who was curled on her tummy. He leaned down to kiss her head lightly, feeling a rush of love. She had turned his life upside down, but how he adored her!

He showered, went to the family room to have a drink and finally returned to his bedroom, where he peeled out of his clothes and stretched out on the bed. Dreading the morning, he fell asleep.

Disoriented, he stirred, rolled over, looked at the alarm and sat up. It was half-past eight. That was the same as waking at two in the afternoon. Megan! He bounded out of bed, yanked on briefs and ran to the nursery. When he flung open the door and looked at her empty bed, he remembered Grace. Grace had Megan. He let out his breath, then sucked it in again as memories and problems tumbled in on him. Today he had to fire Grace.

He sighed and went to his room to bathe, shave and dress, pulling on a white shirt, jeans and boots.

In the kitchen Mrs. Perkins had made coffee and his breakfast. Wearing a denim dress with an apron tied around her waist, she bustled around, getting his plate filled and popping a piece of bread into the toaster for him.

"Good morning, Mr. Sawyer," she said cheerfully, peering at him through her bifocals, and he thought once again how unfortunate that she didn't want the job as nanny. She liked to cook, but said she had taken care of all the babies she wanted to. "I met Miss Talmadge, and she's a nice one. A good nanny for little Megan."

"Yes," he answered, thinking about the task ahead of him. "Thanks for the breakfast. It looks great."

"You missed your sleep last night?" she asked, eyeing him. "I thought your nanny was up with the baby."

"She was, but I was awake, too."

"You'll get back to your regular routine now that you have someone hired. Especially someone young and energetic like she is."

"I hope so."

He ate and then carried a second cup of coffee to his office. With reluctance, he retrieved the nanny applications from the trash and placed them on the middle of his desk. He paged Jett Colby, his foreman, talked to his assistant in California and talked to his office in San Antonio.

Then he sat at his desk and wrote a check to Grace, putting it away in a top drawer. He would break the news to her when Megan went down for her afternoon nap.

Idly he ate a piece of chocolate and stared into space, seeing Grace as she'd looked last night.

Later in the morning when he went to look for Megan, Mrs. Perkins told him that Grace and Megan were outside. It was a balmy day and he stepped out into sunshine. He slipped on his sunglasses and stood watching a moment. Megan had on a sunbonnet, pink ribbons fluttering in the breeze. She was propped and buckled into the baby swing and laughed while Grace pushed her. Grace wore another of her long, nondescript blue skirts and a white cotton shirt, an outfit that looked like a school uniform. Only too well he remembered in exact detail what she looked like under those generic clothes. Her hair was once again fastened behind her head, and the prim schoolmarm was back. But she was only a layer of clothing deep.

That was just as well. He did not want to find her attractive. And he wasn't going through another night like last night. By nightfall, Grace would be packed and out of his life.

He thought about Zoe Elder, the California blonde he'd been dating when his life had turned topsy-turvy with Hank's plane crash. Wyatt realized he could fly Zoe to Texas and cool his libido. The instant he thought of that, he knew he wouldn't. He didn't want a breath of scandal to add to his old reputation. He would wait until he flew to California to see Zoe. He and Megan had three homes now, two in Texas—one in San Antonio and one here— plus his home in California. When he was in California, he could do as he pleased without anyone caring.

"Good morning," he said, walking toward the swing.

"Hi," Grace replied, barely glancing at him.

"Hi, Megan," he said, and she squealed with eagerness.

"Want to take a break?" he asked Grace. "I've got my business taken care of this morning. I'll watch her."

"Thanks. I have some calls I need to make. I won't be long." She hurried to the house and went inside.

"We've got to get you a new nanny," Wyatt told Megan. "One who is much, much older, much less sexy, much less pretty, but just as nice. I know she's out there somewhere. Too bad Grace's mama doesn't want the job. She and her husband could move out here and she could be your nanny."

The idea of a couple held possibilities. Maybe he should advertise for a couple—a man to work on the ranch while his wife was nanny. Too bad none of the men who worked for him now had a wife who wanted to be a nanny—he'd checked that out earlier.

Grace returned shortly and Wyatt left Megan with her while he went back to his office to call Hank's lawyer, Prentice Bolton, and make an appointment. At noon, as Wyatt passed the kitchen, he stopped and went back inside. Grace was feeding Megan. The baby was in her carrier on the kitchen table, with Grace seated in front of her. Grace's mouth was pursed as she watched Megan attempt to take a bite, and Wyatt studied Grace's full, rosy lips, wondering again what it would be like to kiss her. Realizing where his thoughts were going, he moved closer to the table and tried to think about having to fire her.

"Grace, this afternoon when Megan goes down for her nap, will you come see me? I need to talk to you."

"Yes, I will," Grace said, glancing at him.

"I'll be in my office."

She nodded and continued feeding Megan, who had oatmeal in a bowl, on her chin and on her bib. Even so,

Grace was doing a better job of feeding Megan than he usually did. That thought added to his gloom.

Wyatt strode from the room. He raked his fingers through his hair and didn't want to think about having to read through all those nanny applications.

It was half-past two when Wyatt heard a knock on his open office door. He looked up to see Grace.

"Come in," he said, tossing down his pen and leaning back in his chair. "Why don't you close the door?" he suggested, wanting to avoid an interruption by Mrs. Perkins.

"Have a seat," he said, facing Grace across his desk. She sat down, still looking prim. He was amazed at the transformation in her he'd seen last night just by her letting down her hair and changing her clothes. And now he noticed things about her. Her big green eyes he'd remembered, but now in addition to her eyes, he was aware of her rosy skin, her full mouth and the clothing that couldn't hide a tiny waist and full breasts.

"You've been good with Megan."

"She's adorable."

"Thanks. I think so, too. I love her very much. So much that her interests come first in my life." He paused and Grace stared at him with an unwavering gaze. "Grace, I'm sorry, but this is not working out. I'm willing to pay you for your inconvenience and the time you've given me, but I'm going to have to let you go."

He took the check he had written in the morning out of the top drawer of his desk and got up to walk around and hand it to her. "This should cover the trouble I've caused you."

"Why isn't it working out?" she asked without glancing at the check. "I've taken care of Megan, and we get along. I can learn what I need to do for her."

"I know you can, but I was right when I first decided I needed someone older."

"What difference does my age make if I'm doing a good job and she likes me?"

Why had he thought this would be simple? Grace hadn't been simple to deal with since the moment she'd entered his life.

He looked at her. "I think if you stay, things might get much more complicated between us. I'm not looking for a relationship—"

She started laughing and he paused, staring at her. With her green eyes twinkling, she stood and waved away his check. "Keep your check, Mr. Sawyer. And I can go back to calling you mister if it keeps things more formal between us. I have no interest in dating you! Not now, not tomorrow, never!"

"You know, at the risk of sounding egotistical, I can't remember being told that before by any woman. Why not?" Wyatt demanded, feeling oddly disappointed.

"We're not the same type, to say the least! I have plans for my life and goals I want. Someday I would like to marry, but not in the next few years while I'm getting my degree and definitely not you."

"Because of what you've heard about me?"

"Well, yes, that colors it, but…" She smiled at him as if he were a confused child. "I don't want to hurt your feelings, although I sense you've had enough success with women that that can't happen."

"So why don't you want to date me?"

"Your lifestyle is too wild. Frankly, you take a lot of risks. If your reason to let me go is that you don't like the way I care for Megan, then I'll go. But if it's because you think I want to date you, please let's forget that. I'm sure there are a million women you'd rather date than me.''

"And what about last night?" he couldn't resist asking, knowing he was rushing headlong into dangerous waters. "You didn't feel anything when we were together?"

She blinked and as her lips pursed, he could see she was biting back laughter. Wyatt wanted to gnash his teeth in frustration. She was laughing at him again!

"Look, you're experienced and worldly enough to take care of yourself," she said. "I'm definitely not interested in you in any manner other than as my employer, so can we just go back to nanny and employer so I can keep this job?"

"You didn't answer my question," he said, studying her intently. She was saying one thing, but her body language was saying another. Her face was flushed, her words were breathless and he didn't believe her. Yet he hated to think that he couldn't accept a woman telling him she wasn't interested. At the same time, the little minx wanted this job badly—he knew that. And now he was more intrigued than ever. He had expected her to flutter and blush and get coy with him or break into tears and plead for the job, but he hadn't expected her to laugh at him.

"Look, I'm in the habit of being honest," she said. "I would have to be blind and dead not to notice that you are a very good-looking man, Mr. Sawyer. But that's the end of it. Your kitchen is marvelous, but I really don't want it in my apartment. I can work with someone who is attractive without wanting to sleep with him. And I'm sure the same is true for you."

Nanny job or no nanny job, she was interesting him more by the minute.

"I don't believe you."

"As difficult as it may be for your ego to accept this, I'm not interested in you."

"You'll be living here under the same roof with me," he said, "seeing me at night like last night. You don't need to date me to get me aroused and wanting you."

"I'm sorry if that happened last night. Why don't you let me take care of Megan on weeknights? You take the weekends and then we won't cross paths late at night."

This whole interview was going south quickly, and he wasn't sure how she had managed it.

"So I was the only one in that room last night who felt any sparks between us?" he asked softly, moving closer to her. Her eyes widened, and she inhaled swiftly.

"Yes, you were."

"Oh, I think not," he said, moving closer and reaching out to unfasten the barrette that held her hair clipped behind her head. "Let your hair down like it was last night. You don't look like the same woman that way," he continued. "Unfasten that top button so you'll look more like you did last night. Still don't feel anything when I get close?" he asked.

Grace wondered when it had gotten so hot in the room. Her breasts tingled, her mouth had gone dry. Her heart pounded, and she didn't know whether she could get a word out. She felt every brush of his fingers, felt too many reactions, but she wanted to hang on to this job.

"Do you feel anything, Grace?"

"I don't think so," she whispered.

"I think you do. Where's all that blunt honesty of yours now? Tell me when you do feel something. Let's see, if you feel anything when I do this," he said in a husky voice and wrapped his arms around her.

"Mr. Sawyer!"

"The hell with that," he whispered, and leaned down to cover her mouth with his own.

Grace closed her eyes as his arms tightened around her. His tongue played with hers, setting her aflame. She had been less than truthful with him about last night. She had felt sparks all right! Enough to light a bonfire. And the image of him standing naked except for his briefs was indelibly etched in her memory. He was sexy and handsome and irresistible, but she wanted the nanny job desperately. She loved little Megan; the S Bar Ranch was a wonderful place to work, and the pay was fabulous. She definitely didn't want to lose this job.

She tried to stand still, to keep from responding to him, but he tightened his arms and continued to kiss her deeply and thoroughly. He took her breath and curled her toes. Her insides had turned to liquid fire. And all her arguments and thoughts vanished like smoke in wind.

"You don't feel anything yet?" he whispered against her mouth and then went back for yet another deep kiss.

Desire roared as he continued to kiss her, one hand holding her tightly, his other stroking her nape. And then she couldn't resist responding, winding her arm around his neck, returning his kiss, tangling her fingers in his thick hair, letting go completely, forgetting everything else. The world or a job ceased to exist. She was lost, trying to take him with her.

Finally she pushed against him and he straightened, looking at her with a curious intensity that was as disturbing as his kisses.

"All right, so I felt something," she said, trying to find her voice and get some steel into it. "But *you* kissed me. We don't need to kiss. I don't want to, and you don't want to."

She moved away from him, her heart still thudding

while she wondered if she was committing the biggest
folly of her life in arguing to keep her job.

"I can wear clothes that will keep you from noticing
me. You'll find women to date. Neither of us wants a
relationship with each other. Let me keep this job unless
I'm not taking care of Megan the way you want me to.
I promise you'll never see me again like you did last
night."

His silence bothered her as he stood studying her. At
last he said, "I don't think—"

"Look, you can get whatever woman you want. I'm
sure you have all your life. You don't want me. I react
to you, yes, but it means nothing. It's that simple. Let
me do my job and ignore me. I know you can. I'm not
irresistible. Men like you have no interest in women like
me. If we work out a few things about schedules, there
shouldn't be anything difficult in this for you at all. And
I find Megan precious and this job perfect. I want it."

"Whatever happens, be warned now. I am not a marrying man."

Annoyed, she gave him a long look. "Be warned yourself, Mr. Sawyer. No matter how I react to your kisses,
or to you, I don't want to marry you and I'm never going
to."

They glared at each other, and her heart pounded. She
wanted the job and he was the person who could give it
to her or keep her from having it.

"Do I get to be Megan's nanny or not?" she asked as
the silence stretched out.

Four

He was sinking in the quicksand of disaster right up to his eyeballs. He hated the thought of having to interview for another nanny. This one was perfect—or would be if she were fifty years old, married and a granny.

"You said I've done a good job as nanny," she reminded him.

"All right. Stay and we'll see how it goes. During the week you get up at night with Megan. I'll take the weekends—how's that?"

"Fine. I know you're isolated out here. If you'd like to meet some interesting, pretty women, I have some friends who would love to meet you."

"No, I don't think so, Grace," he answered with amusement, thinking there was no time in his entire life he had suffered a shortage of women.

"If you dated, you might be…"

"Might be what?"

Her cheeks turned a bright pink. ''You might notice me less. Although I can dress so you won't notice me at all. I just thought dating might fill a void in your life.''

''No, there's no void. I do date, and Zoe's in California where I was living until I inherited Megan and this ranch.''

''Good! Maybe you can invite Zoe to visit us soon.''

''Maybe so,'' he answered darkly, watching Grace catch her hair and refasten it in the barrette. Wayward tendrils wouldn't stay pinned and sprang loose, curling around her face and reminding him of the softness of her hair, of the softness of her body. Her arms were behind her head, causing her blouse to stretch tightly across her chest and outlining her tempting, full breasts.

Too clearly, the image of Grace as she had looked last night danced into his mind. He drew a deep breath and tried to stop watching her pin her hair, but he couldn't tear his gaze away. If he had a lick of sense, he would fire her now, just yell the words and run out of the room.

Instead, he stood rooted quietly, watching her and re-membering.

She caught him studying her, smiled at him sweetly, giving up catching the feisty locks. ''My hair is a little unruly. I'll go check on Megan. Thank you for letting me keep the job.''

She gave him a big smile and he noticed the dimple in her cheek and the sparkle in her green eyes. She turned and left the room and he watched the sway of her hips until she was out of sight.

''I think I just made the biggest mistake of my life,'' he muttered. How the hell could he not notice her? he asked himself, shaking his head and wiping his forehead.

That evening as he played with Megan, he was acutely aware of Grace sitting quietly on the far side of the family room. She wore her nondescript gray jumper and white cotton blouse. She was pale, devoid of makeup, sitting sedately reading a book while he played with Megan, yet he was as aware of her presence as if she was in a skimpy red swimsuit. When he was close to her, he noticed the sweet, flowery scent that he suspected was purely soap. He wondered if the woman even owned a bottle of perfume. But doing nothing, almost invisible, she was tying him in knots.

Taking a deep breath, he looked at Grace. "I'll put Megan to bed, so go do whatever you'd like for a few hours."

"Thanks, I'm quite happy reading unless I'm disturbing you." She smiled at him and her dimple showed and her green eyes were wide and innocent. Her lips were more inviting than ever.

"No, you're not disturbing me," he lied. "I think I'll take Megan for a walk."

"Tonight?"

"It's a bright moon and she likes the outdoors. I might take her for a ride with me on my horse."

"You'll be careful with her, won't you?"

"Of course, I will," he answered evenly. "I learned to ride almost before I learned to walk, and she will, too."

"That's terribly young to be on a big animal, but you're her daddy now."

It was the first time anyone had told him he was Megan's daddy, and it sounded good. It made him feel warm all over. "I am her daddy now. I'm sorry about Hank and Olivia. Whenever I think about their crash, I'm sorry, but I will be a daddy to Megan, won't I?"

"You already are. She loves you. Look how she smiles when you pick her up."

"You think so?" He looked at the baby on his lap. She lay on his legs with her feet on his stomach while he gently swayed his legs. Megan cooed and watched him and he wondered about her. "You know, I love her more than I've ever loved anyone or anything," he said, forgetting Grace and expressing what he felt. "I've never been around little children and I haven't ever wanted to marry or have children."

"Why on earth not?" Grace asked, her eyes growing round and a frown creasing her smooth brow.

"I don't want to change my lifestyle. I cherish my freedom. And, until Megan, I worried that I'd be like my father. At least, I can lay that worry to rest now." He looked at Grace. "My father was as mean as the devil."

"I'm sorry, Wyatt—Mr. Sawyer," she corrected herself quickly.

"Call me Wyatt. If you stay, we'll be thrown together all day every day a lot of the time. It's Wyatt."

"Well, now you know—you're a good daddy. Look how you are with Megan."

"She's a baby. What will I be like when she's a teenager and driving me crazy?"

"You'll be like you are now—good and kind and loving to her. Look at last night when she was crying constantly. You were as patient as Job with her. You already are a wonderful daddy for your little girl."

Her words wrapped around his heart, causing a lump to form in his throat, and he hated that he was getting emotional. Grace's words, so sweet and wonderful, had gotten to him in a way that years of harshness never had.

He looked at her and met that steady gaze. Most of the time she had him tied in knots and burning with desire. Now she'd melted his heart. He should have fired

her. He stood abruptly, holding Megan in his arms.
"We'll take that walk."

"Oh, good. So you're not taking her on your horse
tonight."

"I might. Grace, I'll take good care of Megan."

She blushed. "I know you will. Sorry, sir," she said,
and he suspected a bit of insolence in that "sir," but she
looked at him with wide-eyed innocence.

He left, striding outside in the cool evening and holding Megan close on his shoulder.

"Baby, you have got some nanny. I wish I'd fired her
today, but you like her and she likes you and she's good
as a nanny, so here she is, driving me crazy. Megan, are
you two females going to end my peaceful life?" He
shifted the baby into the crook of his arm and looked
down into her big brown eyes.

"I know I shouldn't take you on my horse yet—and I
don't intend to, but someday I will. Someday you'll have
your own horse, and we'll ride together whether Nanny
Grace approves or not. C'mon, I'll show you my horse."

Wyatt walked to the pasture that held the horses,
knowing Megan was too little to care or even notice. He
walked back in the moonlight and sat on the porch swing,
swinging her gently until long after her eyes closed.

The next two weeks Wyatt tried to avoid Grace as
much as possible and still see Megan when he got home
from work. Weekends were peaceful, yet by the second
weekend, he missed Grace, who left the ranch on Friday
evening and returned on Sunday evening. He had no idea
where she went.

The first Sunday night in June as she passed the family
room, he called to her. She paused in the doorway. She
wore her gray jumper again and had her hair in a bun,

and he wondered if she'd dressed that way all weekend or just changed to come back to the ranch.

"I have to fly to Dallas tomorrow to close a deal on a hotel I'm selling. Want to bring Megan and come along? We'll be back in the afternoon."

"You want to take both of us with you to Dallas?"

"I have my own plane. I guess you haven't seen the runway, but it's here on the ranch. I'll fly to Dallas and back tomorrow. I thought it would be a good outing for you."

"Wasn't your brother killed flying his own plane?"

"Yes, he was."

"I think Megan and I will stay here. Little babies don't need to be shuffled around, anyway."

"Grace, life is meant to be lived. It's a lot more interesting."

"Maybe, but there's no need to take unnecessary risks. It's none of my business, but I hope that you have a will with a guardian appointed for Megan."

"I'm working on that," he said, studying her, mildly annoyed. "When Megan gets older, I'll take her with me when I fly. And when she gets old enough, I'll teach her to fly."

He could see the disapproval in Grace's expression. "Fine," she said, and turned and left.

"Hells bells," he swore under his breath. And he did have a will. He knew she was right there. It had been a tough decision whether to ask Gabe or Josh about guardianship for Megan, but he had finally asked Josh and Laurie, who had eagerly agreed and seemed flattered that he had asked them.

Two days later Wyatt came home from town. He was hot and tired, wanting to have a cool shower, to stretch out and relax and have a thick steak for dinner. As he went upstairs, he heard laughter.

He paused at the door of Megan's room. The baby was propped against pillows on a blanket on the floor. Grace was on her knees in front of Megan and had her back to the door. She had a pillow in front of her face and was playing peekaboo with Megan.

"Peekaboo!" Grace said, laughing, and Megan laughed out loud, hearty laughter that was irresistible. Wyatt had never heard the baby laugh like that before and he grinned, amused by both of them. Grace leaned over Megan, talking baby talk and blowing her wispy hair, making Megan laugh again, and then Grace snapped the baby's picture.

"That's a girl! We'll surprise your daddy with your pictures. What a cutie you are! Let's have another laugh." The camera vanished and Grace held up the pillow, hiding and then popping out. "Peekaboo!"

Megan laughed again, shaking with it, her brown eyes sparkling while Grace snapped another picture. Wyatt's gaze ran over Grace's bottom and he mentally stripped off the denim skirt. His temperature jumped and he took a deep breath. Then Megan laughed again, another infectious belly laugh.

He went into the room, dropping his coat and tie on a chair.

"I don't know how you do it," he remarked. "I've never made her laugh like that." He dropped down on the floor on his hands and knees beside Grace. "Hi, Megan."

She smiled and cooed at him. He rolled on his back and swung Megan up in his arms, holding her over him, and she squealed with joy, laughing again.

Grace sat back, her legs folded beneath her, while she

raised her camera and focused on them. "Let me get your picture with her." She snapped the shutter. "Now sit up and let me take another one."

Wyatt sat up and held Megan in his arms.

Grace held up the pillow again to hide. "Peekaboo, Megan!" she exclaimed, and when Megan laughed, Grace snapped the picture.

"Okay, now I'll take one of Megan with her nanny," Wyatt said, taking the camera from Grace. She held Megan close, turning the baby to face Wyatt and smiling while Wyatt snapped a picture.

"There." He set aside the camera and took Megan, then lay back on the floor, setting the baby on his chest and playing patty-cake with her. "So what happened today?" he asked, glancing at Grace.

"That's the first I've ever heard her laugh so much," Grace answered. "I took her for a walk outside and then out to play this morning. She loves the outdoors. She had her first chicken-and-noodles today, the baby kind, and she liked that."

Wyatt played with the baby. "It's good to get home."

"How was your day?" Grace asked, and he glanced at her and then back to Megan.

"Rotten. The last years I guess my father let things slip. Then I don't think Hank paid a lot of attention to some of the businesses he had. They were Dad's and I guess Hank was just going through the motions, I don't know. Hank's wife was from a family with more money than ours. Hank really didn't have to work and he might not have wanted to. When he was a kid, he didn't want to work."

"What kind of business do you have?"

"We've got a commercial real-estate business in San Antonio and we've got some bad investments. The books are a mess. I'm getting rid of the accounting firm and getting another one.''

''Too bad I don't already have that degree and training,'' she said lightly. ''Where did you live before you came back here to take care of Megan?''

''Sacramento, California. I still have my home there and my business—and that's commercial real estate, too. I'm still signed up to compete in a rodeo in Sacramento soon. And in July, I'll compete in one in San Antonio.''

''In bull riding, right? I've heard you've won national championships.''

''Yep. I love it.'' He rolled over, gently placing Megan on her back and propping his head on his elbow as he stretched out beside her.

''So you'll run businesses here and in California?'' Grace asked.

''I'm going to have to get rid of something,'' he said while he dangled a rattle for the baby. ''There's too much, and I'd be spread too thin. I'll keep the ones I want, make certain I get good managers.''

''So are you keeping the commercial real estate in San Antonio?''

''Unfortunately, yes. It has some valuable properties, but there are some that my father or Hank should have gotten rid of a long time ago.''

''Who runs this ranch?'' she asked, watching Wyatt with the baby, amazed he wasn't dating constantly. He was the most appealing man she had ever met and he looked adorable, his long length stretched out on the floor, locks of dark hair falling over his forehead as he played with Megan.

''Jett Colby. You probably haven't met him yet, but he's been here for years. He's good, so there's no worry about the ranch. By the way, has Megan been fed?''

"Yes, and she should be ready for bed before long."

"Eat dinner with me," he said quietly.

Surprised, Grace's brows arched. "Thank you," she replied with a smile, "but I think I should say no. Remember, I want to keep my job. I think we should stay professional and keep our distance. Getting to know each other better would be a mistake."

He studied her, wondering about her. He was enjoying her company and he didn't want to eat alone, yet he knew she was right. "Scared we'll start flirting with each other?"

"No," she answered patiently. "I won't flirt."

"Do you ever flirt with guys? Don't you think it's fun to flirt?"

"So far I've never met anyone I wanted to flirt with, because if you do that, you might get to know each other better and get more involved with each other. There hasn't been anyone who interested me that much. Besides, I'm not the flirtatious type."

Since he was thirteen years old, Wyatt had been acutely aware that females were drawn to him. He had never met one who was young, healthy and attractive who hadn't been ready and willing to flirt with him a little.

Grace sat only a few feet from him with the baby between them. Her legs were folded under her, hidden from view, too, by her long skirt.

"Humor me. Come eat with me tonight."

She smiled at him and shifted. "You're a nice employer, and I want to keep it that way—with you as my employer. To do that, we must keep our relationship professional and impersonal. So thank you, but no." She rose gracefully to her feet. "I'll leave Megan with you."

Wyatt watched the sway of her hips as she left the

room and felt disappointed and surprised. Few women, none he could recall, ever turned down invitations from him.

With a sigh he stood and scooped up Megan. "Come with me, sweetie. You'll eat dinner with me, won't you?"

Megan pursed her lips and blew bubbles and Wyatt smiled, kissing her lightly. "You'll eat with me and drool on me and the conversation will be a little lopsided, but at least I can forget the day and play with you."

Two hours later, he hunted for Grace and found her on the porch, a room that was almost all glass and had been built by his grandfather. It was filled with plants, and Grace was curled on a sofa reading a book.

"Hi," he said from the doorway, and she looked up, lowering her book. He held Megan, who was dressed in her pink pajamas, and he himself had changed into a T-shirt and jeans.

"Hi," Grace replied politely.

"Megan slept for about thirty minutes and then woke up. Would you mind watching her for the next hour? Jett called me, and they've got one of the wild bulls and some horses up at the corral. The guys are going to ride them tonight and I want to join them. You can come watch, if you'd like."

"I'll be happy to watch Megan, and maybe we'll come watch you ride. It's certainly nice outside. Why do you have to ride?"

He grinned. "I don't have to. It'll be the most fun I've had this past week."

She shook her head. "I don't know how it could possibly be fun." She took the baby from him, gazing up at him. "But I'm curious enough to come find out, I suppose."

"I just turned the thermostat down again on the air conditioner. I don't think it's working right, but we'll see if it cools down now."

"It's been a little warm today, but we've been outside a lot."

He turned and left. Thirty minutes later Grace headed with Megan toward the corral, where a bunch of cowboys sat on the fence or stood watching. At her approach, a sandy-haired man jumped down and strolled to her, holding out his hand.

"Jett Colby, Miss Talmadge. I'm Wyatt's foreman."

"Glad to meet you. I thought I'd come watch. The baby likes to be outside."

"She's a cutie. It'll be safer if you don't sit on the fence like the guys are. They don't have a baby in their arms and they can jump for safety when they need to. Just stand over there in the shade of that cottonwood and you can see plenty."

"Thanks," she said, smiling at him.

In minutes she saw why she shouldn't sit on the fence as they opened a gate and Wyatt came out on a bucking bull that looked enormous to Grace. The dun-colored animal had long horns, jumped into the air and came down stiff-legged, only to twist and buck again. Cowboys yelled and cheered while Wyatt clung to the bull with one hand. She couldn't look, turning away. After a few seconds she turned back and saw him still riding the beast.

When at last he bounded off the bull, Wyatt landed with both feet to wild cheers from the cowboys watching. The bull turned to charge him and Wyatt ran, leaping on the fence and springing over it to drop down on the other side. Cowboys sprang down, scrambling to get out of the way of the angry bull, which pawed the ground and snorted.

Wyatt came striding over to her. "Hi."

Grace gazed up at him. He looked exhilarated, far more relaxed and happy than he had when he'd come home from work today, and she realized he thrived on the bull ride and probably on the other wild things he did.

"How can you do that?"

"It's great. Makes you feel alive."

"I'd think it would make you want to stay alive and avoid moments like that again."

He laughed as he peeled off leather gloves. "I'm thirsty. Let's go up to the house and get something cold to drink. I'll take Megan now. Believe me, on the back of that bull, I forget all about lousy bookkeeping and money-losing properties."

"I'll carry her. You look dusty."

"Aw, she'll wash. Give me my sweet baby," he said, grinning and taking Megan from Grace. "When Megan gets older, I'll want you to bring her to watch me ride in rodeos. Will you do it?"

"We'll see when the time comes," Grace replied. "You're her sole parent now. Do you think you ought to take such risks?"

"Bull riding? It isn't that risky. The odds are better than when you get in your car and drive down the highway."

"I don't think you'll convince me of that one."

"What do you do to relax, Grace?"

She glanced up at him. Locks of black hair fell on his forehead and sweat beaded his face. She had to hurry to keep up with his long, easy stride. "I read a good book."

"That's mighty quiet."

"I told you—we're worlds apart. You wouldn't enjoy spending most of your spare moments reading, and I wouldn't enjoy your motorcycle or your bull riding."

"You don't like life on the wild side?"

"It's never been the way I or any of my family have lived. Besides, you have responsibility now."

"Megan? I'll be careful."

"Why do you like all these wild activities?"

He shrugged and reached to open the back gate for her, stepping aside to let her go ahead. "They're exciting. They make me feel more alive. They're a challenge and I like challenges," he said, looking at her intently, and suddenly Grace suspected he was talking about her, yet common sense said he couldn't possibly be referring to her.

"Were your brothers like you?"

"They liked the wild stuff, if that's what you mean. I think maybe we all started in defiance of our dad—or to get his attention. Then I found I liked doing the things that I did, so I've continued." He leaned closer to her. "And I've never told anyone that before. But then, no one has ever asked me why I do what I do. A lot of women are impressed by daredevil antics like bull riding and skydiving. But you're not, are you?"

"Mostly I'm a little horrified. I'll have to think about taking Grace to a rodeo, but by then you'll be older and maybe wiser."

He laughed and looked down at the sleeping baby in his arms. "I'll go put her down and then fix us cold drinks."

"Give her to me and I'll put her down while you fix the cold drinks," Grace said, reaching up and taking Megan from him.

Her hands brushed his and his chest, and she was

aware of each contact, but hoped he never knew. She held Megan close and left, knowing if she had any sense, she wouldn't go back, but she was enjoying his company and she wanted that cold drink.

When she came down the stairs, she could hear Wyatt swearing. He stood in the hall beside the thermostat.

"What's wrong?" she asked.

Five

"Haven't you noticed? It's hotter in this house than it is outside. The air conditioner isn't working or the thermostat isn't working. The air conditioner is probably old as Methuselah and I'll have to replace it, but that won't do any good tonight."

He had a screwdriver in hand, and part of the thermostat was in pieces on a table beside him while he worked on the remainder.

"Want me to fix something to drink?"

"Yeah. I want a cold beer. Can you hand me that little silver screw?"

She found what he wanted and handed it to him. He tried to insert it into a tiny hole, but wires were in his way. She reached up to hold the wires so he could work. He glanced at her.

"Thanks. I'm on fire," he said, turning the screwdriver until he had the screw in place. "You can let go now."

He yanked off his T-shirt, wiped the sweat off his forehead and tossed the shirt aside, turning his back to her as he did so.

She drew a deep breath, looking at the scars on his back.

"You've got scars," she said quietly. At first sight, she thought he'd been hurt from some of the wild things he'd done, but then she realized that wasn't what caused them.

"Yeah, thanks to my old man," he said, and bitterness laced his voice. He looked at her. "It doesn't matter now. I got over letting him hurt me badly a long, long time ago, but I live with those scars."

"I'm sorry," she said, appalled that he'd had a monster for a parent and no mother.

He shrugged. "It's over, and he's dead." Wyatt bent over the thermostat. "I don't think this thermostat is the problem," he said, putting it back together. "I may have to replace the air conditioner, but we'll have to suffer through tonight." He put the cover on the thermostat and looked upstairs. "It'll be hot as Hades up there. We can go into town to the house there, but we'll have to pack, drive in and cool it down. Or we can go to a hotel. Or let's sleep in the yard. I can get cots."

The thought of sleeping in the yard with Wyatt only a few feet away sent a shock through her system, but a hotel sounded worse. "We can't go out there and leave Megan inside."

"No. I'll move her crib outside."

"You can't do that."

"Sure, I can. Sleeping outside will be the easiest thing to do. I'll get it moved now, and we can take turns with her while I get the cots up. Come help me and I'll move the crib. We'll get the cold drinks in a minute."

As they entered the baby's room, Wyatt motioned to Grace. "You carry Megan. I'll take the mattress down and then come back for the crib."

Grace picked up the baby. Megan was indeed warm, her black hair in wet ringlets against her head. She snuggled into Grace's arms, but never opened her eyes. Grace went downstairs, waiting to hold the door for Wyatt.

He came right behind her with the mattress tucked under his arm and they went outside where the air was cooler now and a slight breeze had sprung up.

"I'll get the crib," he said. "I can't believe she's sleeping through this."

"She was outside a lot today. I think that wears her out." Grace sat on the porch swing and gently moved it back and forth.

In minutes Wyatt stepped through the back door with the pieces of the crib. Grace marveled that he had taken it apart so quickly. She watched him reassemble it beneath the long branches of one of the oaks. Moonlight spilled over him, highlighting the play of muscles in his arms and back as he worked. Grace drew a deep breath. Wyatt was unbelievably handsome, with broad shoulders, a narrow waist and well-toned muscles. How was she going to sleep only a few feet from him tonight? She couldn't imagine getting ten minutes' sleep.

When he put the mattress in place and waved his hand, she picked up Megan and strolled over to the crib.

"All ready for my little princess," he said.

"Very nice, Wyatt. You're handy."

"That's a new one. I've been told I'm a lot of things, but handy…well, I don't think so. 'Course, I haven't had many air conditioners break on me, either. Now I'll finally get those cold drinks. What'll you have?"

"Just soda pop. Any kind."

He returned in minutes with a cold beer and a glass of pop over ice for her. He had a box of chocolates in hand. "Want a piece of candy?" he asked, and she shook her head.

"No, thanks. And how you eat those with beer, I'll never know."

"I'm a man of complexities," he said, and she smiled.

"When Megan gets to toddling, you'll have to put your chocolates up high."

"I will. I know they're not good for her. We weren't ever allowed to have candy at the ranch. From the time I've been on my own, I've had chocolates on hand. But it isn't out of spite. I love chocolate—it's the next best thing to kissing a pretty woman."

"Well, Mr. Sawyer, I don't care for chocolate and I wouldn't know about the other," she replied, and he grinned.

"Are you trying to remind me that I'm your employer and to drop the talk about kissing?"

"I knew you'd get it."

He grinned. "I'll sit with Megan now and you go do what you have to do inside. Then you can sit with her. I can tell you, I'm taking a cold shower before I turn in."

As Grace walked away, he raised the bottle and drank, lowering it and sitting in a lawn chair, in a moment reaching for a chocolate.

Even with the tree giving them leafy shadows, moonlight made the yard almost as bright as early evening. Down at the corral lights were on and cowboys were still riding, still cheering and clapping, the sounds muted by distance.

Wyatt sat in the cool breeze and peeled off his boots and socks. He raked his fingers through his hair and thought about the evening. Grace disapproved of his bull riding. She probably disapproved of most everything he did. And she was right—they were entirely different, yet what was it about her that had him opening himself up to her? He had told her things tonight he had never told anyone else. She was a listener deluxe, fixing those big green eyes on him and hanging on every word. Earlier, it had been a relief after an insufferable day to come home to laughter and Grace's quiet questions and interest.

And she wouldn't eat dinner with him. How many women had turned down the offer of dinner? He couldn't think of any, yet again, he wondered if his ego had gotten blown up through the years of easy conquests. He'd told her he liked challenges; what he didn't tell her was that she was a challenge. One he knew he should ignore, but how tempting to want to storm the walls she'd put up between them. He remembered when he'd kissed her and how finally she'd kissed him back.

He inhaled deeply, knowing he should try to keep a lid on that memory. Her kisses were hotter than fire. Was she a virgin? Something he hadn't dealt with since he was a kid. "And you're not going to have to deal with it now," he said to himself.

"Are you talking to me?" she asked.

He turned and stared at her. Her hair was fastened in a bun behind her head and she wore sweats. He stood up and looked fully at her.

"Have you lost your mind or are you sick? You're in sweats when it's probably ninety degrees right now."

"We're sleeping out here together, more or less. I told you I would wear clothes that would prevent—"

"Great grief, woman! Go put on something cool! I'm not going to jump you."

Even in the darkness, he could see her chin lift and

see her draw herself up. "I know you're not," she replied evenly, "but I promised you that day that I would dress so you wouldn't notice me."

"I won't notice you if you come back in a swimsuit, I promise. Just go get cool before you pass out, and I have to take those heavy clothes off you myself."

That sent her running. He could imagine the sparks shooting from those green eyes. He sat down and took another long swallow of beer. He thought about the short nightie she'd worn the first night. He had lied six ways of Sunday when he'd told her he wouldn't notice what she was wearing, but he'd try. And he'd bet the ranch she didn't come back in the nightie. Cutoffs and a T-shirt, maybe, although, except for the nightie, he had never seen her in anything that revealing.

In minutes she returned, coming across the yard in the moonlight in a knee-length cotton skirt and a T-shirt. And he was glad he was sitting in the shadows, because he couldn't keep from staring. The T-shirt molded full breasts that bounced slightly with each step she took. And the shirt was tucked into a tiny waist. He already knew about her tiny waist. And the skirt halfway revealed her fabulous legs. In those clothes she wouldn't go into melt-down, although peeling her out of the sweats had been tempting. He knew he better stop staring, but it was difficult to pull his gaze away.

Miss Goody Talmadge didn't approve of him. And his bull riding tonight had been another mark against him, so he should pay no attention to her except as his nanny. Straitlaced and virginal, she wasn't his type. Although her kiss hadn't been virginal. He glanced over his shoulder again and stood.

"That's better," he said, still thankful for the darkness because she couldn't see that he was staring. This time her hair was piled on her head in a mass of curls with loose strands falling around her face. She was really quite good-looking, and ninety percent of the time she hid it well.

"If you'll stay with Megan, I'll go get the cots now. And have my cold shower."

"Take your time," she said, moving a lawn chair slightly farther from the one he had been sitting in. She sat down, crossed her legs and took a sip of her cold pop. Then she looked up at him, and he realized he had been watching her every move. He could sense disapproval and he turned and left.

"Leave the woman alone," he whispered to himself as he crossed the porch. But he needed that cold shower because he had been thinking about her kiss, looking at her, fantasizing about her, and he was hotter than ever.

He took his time under the shower and tried to get his mind on business, on going back to California. He thought about Zoe and felt little interest. He hadn't called her for days, hadn't even returned her calls. Had their relationship been so shallow that he no longer missed it or cared? Now that he stopped to think about it, he realized he didn't care. And he needed to let Zoe know. He hadn't called her since he'd hired Grace. Sheer coincidence. He had no romantic interest in Grace, and it wouldn't matter if he did, because she wouldn't let him get within two feet of her again.

He dressed in fresh jeans and switched off the lights, going to the kitchen to get Grace another cold pop and himself a second cold beer.

He strolled across the lawn. Grace had her long legs propped on a yard chair and her shoes off. Her back was to him, and he couldn't see her face.

"I brought you another cold drink," he said when he

reached her. He held it out, and her fingers brushed his when she took it.

"Thanks," she said, sitting up and slipping her feet into her shoes.

"You can go barefoot around me," he remarked with amusement.

He pulled his chair closer to hers and turned it slightly to face her. He knew he disturbed her and she kept up a constant guard around him, but the more standoffish she was, the more he was tempted to try to break through her defenses.

"Am I bothering you?"

"No, you're not," she said. "When is the woman you date going to come to Texas to see you?"

"I'm going to break things off with her. Now that we have time and distance between us, I realize I'm not really interested. I'll call her tomorrow."

"That's good because she's been calling you about twice a day lately."

"You don't approve of anything about me, do you."

"Oh, yes, I do! You're a wonderful daddy for Megan. I don't think you could be a better dad."

"Thank you," he answered quietly. "That means a lot to me," he added, feeling pleased beyond measure. "I didn't have a role model.... Well, in a way I did. My friends' fathers were both role models. Gabe's dad was good to me and Josh's dad let me live with them for long periods of time. Josh's dad is the one who stopped the beatings. After a particularly bad one, he came over and warned my father not to lay a hand on me again. Josh's dad was full of life, but he had his moments when he could be earnest. He wasn't as large as my father, but he must have thrown a scare into the old man, because that was the last beating I received from him."

Grace reached out to touch Wyatt's wrist. "I'm sorry. My family is so loving I can't even begin to imagine what your life was like." Her hand was light and warm on his wrist, the slightest touch, yet he felt it in every nerve in his body.

"It's just as difficult for me to imagine what your life was like," he said, wanting to cover her hand, but restraining himself. She moved her hand away.

"My family was always close," she continued. "We never had a lot of money—maybe that's why money is important to me, although it isn't to the rest of my family. My dad was a minister, and then when we got older, he and my mom both wanted to devote their lives to missionary work. They've been out of the country on missions most of the time since I was thirteen. They took us with them until I got older. I've lived in Mexico, Bolivia and Peru."

"Ever been in love?"

"Not really," she said.

"You don't feel like you're missing out on life?"

"By not being in love? Hardly."

"Your parents have a good marriage from what you've told me. Don't you want what they've had?"

"Sure, someday, but not right now. I'm young and I have plans. That second night I was here, you said you valued your freedom. Well, I value mine."

"All right, what about just being in love for the thrill of it? Life's a lot more of an adventure when you're in love."

"I think you thrive on excitement. I thrive on contentment."

"Tell me about your life in Mexico and Bolivia and Peru," he said, curious about her.

Grace talked quietly, then asked him about his life in California.

"You didn't answer me before—you don't approve of me, do you, Grace."

"I told you, I think you're a wonderful daddy for Megan."

"But you wouldn't eat with me tonight because you disapprove of my lifestyle, right?" he persisted, leaning forward and putting his elbows on his knees, narrowing the distance between them.

"We agreed to keep our distance since I'm your employee. I think I should stick with that," she replied coolly, but he noticed she licked her lips and sounded breathless when she spoke.

"You wouldn't stick with it if I asked you to do something with me and you wanted to be with me, now would you?"

"I suppose you're right."

"So it gets back to disapproval." He sighed and sat back in his chair. "That's okay. I've been surprised how friendly people in town are. Life changes, people change and money makes a difference. I think they like the Sawyer money enough to overlook my past. If you like money so much, I'm surprised that doesn't work for you."

"Money's important, but it's not that important to me."

He laughed softly. "So if I asked you out, you'd turn me down."

"Definitely, but I don't think you're really going to ask me out. I'd turn you down because I'm your nanny."

"Suppose you weren't my nanny. Would you go out with me then?"

"Tell me about all those businesses you inherited,"

she said. "What are you keeping and what are you disposing of?"

"I don't know yet," he answered, amused by her efforts to change the subject. She wouldn't go out with him under any circumstances. She was his nanny, and the heat must be getting to him because he shouldn't want to ask her out or ask her to join him for dinner or even spend the evening talking to her.

"Gabe's told me about the rumors in town," he said, knowing he shouldn't care, but wanting her approval. "Grace, I don't have any kids running around Stallion Pass."

She turned to look at him. "I didn't think you did. Those rumors sounded a little farfetched. If what I heard was true, you'd have a whole passel of kids."

"Nope. None. I've never fathered a child."

She looked at him sharply and he gazed back, guessing what was in her thoughts.

"I know all the stories, and you've heard why I left town."

"Yes, I have. They say that you left because you got someone pregnant."

"The girl who was involved died that summer in a swimming accident."

"I've heard that, too."

"Besides the girl involved," he said, "there were four others of us who knew the truth. Hank, Gabe, Josh and me. So now only two besides me. With Hank and Olivia gone, it no longer matters much. Hank was the father."

Startled, Grace stared at him, and he gazed back at her. "Your brother was the baby's father? Why would you tell everyone it was your baby?"

"Hank and Olivia were engaged. Olivia was a San Antonio socialite, and Hank was afraid if the truth came out, it would end their engagement. They had this big wedding planned, and Hank wanted to marry Olivia. He was afraid that if Olivia and her family learned about the pregnancy, there wouldn't be a wedding.''

"And you did that for your brother?''

"Yeah, I did,'' he said gruffly. "It wasn't that big a deal. Everyone believed the worst about me, anyway, and most of the time I deserved it. I did a lot of wild things. I earned the reputation I had, but I never got anyone pregnant. My father was making my life miserable. I told Hank I'd take the heat because I was ready to get out of town, anyway.''

Grace still stared at him in amazement. "That's really something—to bear people's anger for your brother. So you were close to your brother?''

"Yeah, as close as I've been to anyone in my family. Hank and I fought and we weren't alike, but we got along. I didn't want his engagement broken, so I didn't mind.''

"With the exception of your two close friends and your brother, you've never told anyone this, have you.''

"Nope, I haven't. I guess I care what you think about me. That doesn't happen often,'' he said, taking another long swallow of beer.

Grace felt a mixture of surprise and relief that he wasn't as terrible as she'd been told, and another feeling, a closeness, because he'd opened himself up to her and shared what must have been his deepest secret. She couldn't ignore the rush of pleasure when he'd said he cared what she thought about him.

"People in Stallion Pass will always think you were the father.''

"Doesn't matter. Like you said, you know yourself, your family—in my case, my brother—knows you, your friends know you and no one else matters. I've felt that way since I was a kid. My best friends, Gabe and Josh, knew the truth. They were the only ones who mattered to me. And as far as I know, she did die in a swimming accident. I know there were rumors of murder, but that was all they were, rumors. I was riding in a rodeo that night and Hank was with Olivia at a party. It was all a long time ago.''

''What did you do when you left here?''

''Odd jobs. The first summer I worked in an oil field because it paid well. I worked on ranches, gentled wild horses, rode in rodeos, hit a lot of bars and did a lot of partying and ended up in California.'' He took another swallow of beer.

''What did you do in California?''

''I began to make big money with my bull riding and met a man who talked me into going to work for him in commercial real estate. I knew a little about it because of my father's businesses here. I used the money from bull riding to get into the real-estate business. I took classes, took the tests, got my license and became a broker. That guy taught me all about the business, and when he retired, I bought his business. I got in when property was cheaper, and then prices shot up and I made a lot of money. I made good investments and made more money.''

''So commercial real estate is your first love.''

''Hell, no. It's just a good way to make money.''

''What's your first love?''

He grinned and set down his bottle and leaned toward her again, resting his elbows on his knees. ''Pretty women. We've talked enough about me. What's your first love, Grace?''

''I'm the nanny, remember. If I had a room that was

air-conditioned, I'd go to it now. Let's keep this impersonal."

"Scared of me?"

"No, I'm scared of losing my job. And I made some
promises to you about that."

"So you did and you've kept them, but let's just enjoy
the summer night and conversation. I promise, you won't
lose your job over us tonight. You're a very good
nanny."

"Thanks."

"So what's your first love?" he asked again, leaning
closer and running a finger along her arm.

"Books, probably. Mr. Sawyer, you need to keep your
distance. I don't want to have to go inside."

"Don't even think about going into that hot house.
And I would keep my distance if I thought I was repul-
sive to you, but I don't think that's the case."

Grace's pulse was racing and she was thankful for the
darkness so he couldn't see what kind of reaction he was
getting from her. She leaned forward so that she was only
inches from his face, looking him straight in the eye. "I
think you're interested in me solely because I've said no
to you. If I had gone all starry-eyed and eaten dinner
with you and if I'd hung on every word you said and
flirted with you, I don't think you'd be sitting out here
talking to me now, nor would you give me five minutes
of your time. You're just interested because I haven't
been in a swoon over you, Wyatt Sawyer."

"Maybe there's some truth in what you say, but that's
not why I asked you to join me for dinner tonight. When
I got home from work, I was enjoying your company,
and I'd had a lousy day that you were making me forget.
And nanny or not, sparks fly when we're together. You

have to be as aware of that as I am. Deny that one, Grace.''

''I will deny it. I don't think there are sparks every time we're together. There's nothing now. Bulletin for you: I'm not interested. I find it difficult to pretend, and even if I did pretend, I don't care to be another conquest, someone you get bored with after a while.''

''No sparks, huh?'' he asked, his deep voice like velvet. He slipped his hand behind her head and looked at her mouth. ''You don't feel anything?''

''Nothing,'' she said calmly, and started to pull away. His hand tightened and he leaned closer, his lips brushing hers.

''Scared of me?''

''Not at all,'' she replied calmly, but her pulse jumped and she could feel the sparks and the contest of wills. Her heart thudded, and she wondered if he could hear it. She didn't want to feel anything. She didn't want to be a summer conquest because he was stuck on the ranch with his new responsibility and bored with life, burdened with having to settle his brother's estate. But how impossible it was to sit quietly, to try to avoid responding to his light kisses, to try to keep her wits about her.

''Nothing yet, Grace?'' he whispered, pausing to look at her. His bedroom eyes would have sent her pulse skyrocketing without kisses. Add his to-die-for kisses, and fire raged in her veins.

He kissed her again, this time his mouth settling on hers, opening hers. As his tongue stroked hers, he lifted her easily onto his lap, his arm encircling her waist and pulling her close against him.

Her insides melted, and her resistance was gone, yet she fought to hang on to wisdom and to refrain from kissing him in return. But without thought she had wrapped her arm around his neck. She was pressed against his bare chest, and her body was having a different reaction from her brain.

She shifted away from him, looking at him. "See? Nothing. I'm not a sexy woman and I'm not exciting to men. Forget it." Guilt and desire besieged her. Had she ever told a whopper like that one? She could barely breathe, her heart still pounded, and she wanted to throw her arms around him and kiss him for the rest of the night.

She was trying to get off his lap. His chest expanded as he exhaled and his arm tightened around her waist. "You are sexy and you are exciting and there's no way I'm going to give up now." He kissed her again, throwing himself totally into it, his tongue taking possession.

Her pulse roared in her ears, and she felt devoured, on fire. How much resistance could she keep up? His kisses obliterated the world and ignited her deepest desires. She had never been kissed like this. His kisses stormed her barricades and demolished them. He possessed, demanded and won her response.

As she kissed him in return, she moaned softly, heard herself only dimly. Angry with herself, annoyed with him, she suddenly wanted to devour that impenetrable self-assurance of his.

She was on his lap and she felt his thick shaft press against her hip. Their kisses were escalating, and his breathing was as ragged as hers. Her fingers wound in his thick hair. Her breasts tingled and she felt a low throbbing ache deep inside her.

When his fingers trailed lightly along her bare thigh, she shook with pleasure. She knew she was committing folly, risking her job, her future, yet how could she stop kisses that turned her inside out and sent her pulse galloping?

Then he framed her face with his hands. She opened her eyes to look at him and met a solemn gaze.

''Now you feel something, don't you?'' he asked.

Six

"**H**ow can I keep from feeling something? You're the expert, and I've had very little experience. But I didn't invite your kisses and that was next to force—"

"Force!" he exclaimed, sounding appalled. "Grace, I have never used force in my life. Here—hands behind my back. Resist if you don't feel anything." He put his hands at his sides, releasing her, but he leaned forward to brush kisses on her throat up to her ear, his tongue tracing her ear and then trailing kisses to her mouth where he brushed his lips across hers again. Her insides were wound tight and she wanted to hold him and kiss him, and she wanted him to hold her tightly as he had been and kiss her as he had been kissing her. She knew the word *force* had been unfair, but to hang on to her self-control and not become mush in his arms, she had to use whatever tactics she could.

"Go on, Grace, stop me if you don't like this. I'm not

holding you. There's no force whatsoever," he whispered between kisses, trailing them around to the side of her neck, then back to her mouth.

She couldn't stop him. She wanted to resist, but she couldn't. "I know you didn't use force," she whispered, hopelessly lost. She kissed him, yielding, tightening her arm around his neck and leaning closer, kissing him with all her pent-up passion.

Then his arms wrapped around her and crushed her against him, and he kissed her long and deeply. His body was hot and hard and his kisses were fiery.

Finally she wriggled and slipped off his lap, moving swiftly back to her chair. Both of them were gulping for air as they stared at each other.

"We've got to stop, Mr. Sawyer. I'm your employee," she said, emphasizing the last word.

He hitched his chair close to hers, facing her, his index finger trailing circles on her knee. "Stop that 'Mr. Sawyer' stuff. It's Wyatt. You're a desirable woman."

She took a deep breath and stared at him. He trailed his fingers along her throat. "Your pulse is skyrocketing. Go out with me Saturday night."

She shook her head. "I can't keep from responding to your kisses, but you know we shouldn't take this further. Thank you about Saturday, but I'm sorry, no."

He stared at her and ran his fingers through his hair. "Why shouldn't we? There's no law that says a guy can't date his nanny."

"We shouldn't date because we're not the least compatible. We're as different as ice and fire. You don't like the things I enjoy, and I don't like the things you enjoy. I don't approve of the risks you take. I hear you at night, riding away on your motorcycle, and I've seen you—you go very fast. You like riding wild animals, you like a lot of daredevil things. Now you have a responsibility to Megan. You're her father now.''

He looked away and ran his fingers through his hair again. ''Hank didn't change his lifestyle, and he was her real daddy. I don't think I take giant risks. I can cut back on skydiving, but the other stuff isn't that dangerous. Anyway, that really doesn't have a whole lot to do with our going out Saturday night.''

''Do you not understand the word *no?*''

He grinned and ran his finger along her cheek and then leaned forward to kiss her briefly and lightly, yet setting her heart pounding again. He stopped abruptly and placed his hand against her throat. ''Your reaction is why I don't want to take no for an answer from you. If fireworks didn't go off when I kissed you, I wouldn't care or be interested.''

''Find someone else, and don't kiss me. Now, do I have to move into the hot house?''

He smiled at her. ''Nope. I know when I'm not wanted. I'll go join the guys for a while.'' He leaned close. ''But someday, Grace, you'll say yes to me,'' he said in that husky, velvety voice that was a caress in itself. ''Half of you already has.''

He stood and strode away toward the corral, and she watched his easy, long-legged stride. It had taken every bit of willpower she possessed to turn down a date with him Saturday night. She ached to go out with him, to kiss him more, to have him kiss her. Wyatt was exciting, sexy, appealing and nice. She had never dated a man like him. But she knew she was doing the right thing. If she wasn't careful, she was going to be in love with her handsome boss. Even if they both wanted a deep relationship, there was no future for them. She couldn't bear his wild hobbies, and he wouldn't be able to settle for her quiet life.

She stood and moved to the crib to look at the sleeping baby. Pulling her cot closer to the crib, Grace stretched out and lay looking at the stars and thinking about Wyatt. She knew sleep wasn't going to come, possibly for hours.

She had no idea how late it was when she heard Wyatt returning. She sat up to see if it was him.

"Grace?" he said softly.

"I'm awake."

"I'm going to shower and then I'll be back. Want a break from staying with Megan before I go inside?"

"No, I'm fine."

He passed her and she turned to watch him walk toward the house. Moonlight spilled over him and she saw a jagged, bleeding cut across his shoulder and back.

"Wyatt, are you hurt?"

"I was dodging a flying hoof and didn't quite get clear. I'm okay."

"I can't leave Megan, but bring something to put on that cut after you shower and I'll help you."

"It's okay," he said as he headed toward the house.

In half an hour he was back and she sat up, swinging her feet off the cot.

"Did you bring something to put on your cut?"

"No, I didn't. I don't need anything."

"Stay with Megan, and I'll go get it."

"Here," he said with resignation in his voice. He held out a small spray bottle and a dry washcloth. "I thought you might insist on getting something, but I don't need this."

"Turn around and sit," she said, looking at the long gash across his back. "This may hurt, but you need to put some antiseptic on that cut. It looks terrible."

She opened the bottle and sprayed it, dabbing at his back where the antiseptic ran. He had one deep cut and several smaller cuts across his muscular back. He sat without flinching, yet she knew it had to hurt.

"All done."

"Why can't you sleep?" he asked, turning to look at her. She sat in one of the lawn chairs again and faced him.

"I don't know."

"Liar," he said softly. "You can't sleep for the same reason I can't."

"Maybe, but we're not going to do anything about it."

"Okay, we'll sit and talk, but there are better ways to spend time. Tell me what you want out of life. You don't care about dating, so what do you want?"

"Eventually I want a family. For the past few years I've been concentrating on my education."

"Turn around and I'll give you a back rub. That'll help you relax and go to sleep," he said.

"I don't—"

"Turn around. It's just a back rub," he said. Grace turned her back to him and he scooted his lawn chair close behind her. She knew she should argue with him and avoid any physical contact, yet a back rub seemed ridiculous to argue about.

His hands began to gently massage her shoulders. She became aware of his knees on either side of her and realized he was sitting quite close behind her and she sat between his legs.

"You're taking accounting. What do you want out of that? If you have money, what will you do with it?"

"I want to own my own home. My parents have never owned a home."

"No kidding?" he asked, and she could hear the surprise in his voice.

"No. Dad was a minister and Mom was a choir director and a lay minister. They moved and lived in houses furnished by the church. Then when they started going on missions, they sure didn't need a house here. They still live in church housing wherever they are.''

"I hadn't thought about that. Except for the years in California, I've been on this ranch all my life. My great-great-grandfather built this place. I own my home in California, and now I've inherited Hank's San Antonio home and this place.''

"Wyatt, are you going to live here or in San Antonio or in California?''

"Probably here and sometimes in San Antonio. I'll spend time off and on in California, but I'm not moving back out there to stay. I like Texas too much.''

"Where will Megan go to school? In San Antonio?''

"I hadn't thought about it yet. She'll probably start school in Stallion Pass like I did.''

"If that's the case, you should socialize with young couples who have little children so Megan will have friends to play with.'' Grace turned to look at him. "If you had a wife, she would get to know other mothers around here. You already have some close friends. I think you ought to have a party, have people out here who have young children and make some friendships for Megan's sake. She's the one who is isolated.''

"I hadn't thought about it, but I guess you're right.''

"Do you go to church?''

"Church never has been much in my life. It sure wasn't growing up.''

"Maybe you should attend one, so Megan will have that in her life, too. Then she'll know kids through church.''

Grace had turned around again, and Wyatt kneaded her back, working lightly, too aware of her fine bones, her slender body, wanting to slide his hands a few more inches around her and cup her full, tempting breasts. He knew if he did, he'd probably lose a nanny. He was only half thinking about what she was discussing, yet he realized she was right.

"Maybe I should have a party, but what'll I do with Megan, and suppose no one comes?"

"People will come. You said yourself that people had been nice in Stallion Pass. You're sexy, appealing, established, wealthy—they won't turn you down. And your close friends will come for sure. As for Megan, I'll be there to take care of her, and you can show her off. No one can resist a sweet little baby. Let everyone bring their children. That's more fun, anyway, and this house looks able to take kids."

"I'm sexy and appealing?"

"Don't push it, Wyatt. You know you are."

He grinned. "So if you and I have a party, what about rumors starting about us?"

She glanced over her shoulder at him, giving him a smile. He knew she didn't mean to, but it was a provocative pose and he had to fight to keep from sliding his arms around her waist and pulling her close. Instead, he tried to pay attention to what she was telling him.

"Don't be ridiculous. No one will notice me. I promise, you won't have any problems about rumors."

"You'll help me plan this?"

"Sure," she said, turning around again.

He rubbed her shoulders, his thumbs gently massaging her nape, and then he worked his hands down her back, his imagination stripping her bare.

She scooted her chair away. "Thanks, Wyatt. I'd offer to give you a back rub in return, but you're too cut up."

"I'm not cut all over and it's been a tedious day. I'll

take you up on that rub.'' He turned his chair around. His interminable day had ended when he'd stepped into the nursery this afternoon with Megan and Grace, but he wanted Grace's hands on him.

In seconds her hands began to knead his left shoulder, carefully avoiding his injury. Her slightest touch caused a jump in his pulse, and the back rub was making his breath catch and his heart pound. He was amazed by the effect she had on him. Too easily, she could tie him in knots. He'd had experience with women since too far back to remember, so why was Grace with her light touches, her reluctant presence, her standoffishness, keeping him tied in knots? Why did he want her so badly?

Was it a perverse streak in him for conquest? He didn't think so. He thought it was a scalding mutual attraction that she felt far more than she would admit to him. She was right about making friends with locals for Megan's sake. He needed to have a network of friends because Megan could easily be isolated if he stayed on the ranch.

On the other hand, he could move to San Antonio and put Megan in private school, and a lot of the social problems would solve themselves.

''Wyatt, earlier you said the real-estate business isn't your first love, but you never answered me about what *is* your first love.''

''This ranch. I missed it like hell when I left. I love it.''

''Then why don't you sell the businesses you don't want and get someone competent to run the commercial real estate for you? Take over the ranch. It's yours now.''

''Jett's totally capable of running this place.''

''It isn't big enough for the two of you?''

He could hear the incredulity in her voice. ''Well, a

lot of the time, yes, it is. But there are decisions that he makes that I would if I came back.''

"Have you talked to him? He might be ready for you to take charge. How old is Jett?"

"Early fifties, I think. He's the one person on this ranch my dad didn't mess with."

"He might be ready to let up a little. Some of this looks like hard, physical work."

"It is, and I think that's why I like it," Wyatt replied, wondering about Jett and if he might not mind stepping down a little. Wyatt thought about the ranch and knew he would love to have it as his full-time work.

Grace's hands were at the small of his back, rubbing and kneading, and the effect was far from relaxing. "Thanks, Grace," he said, and pulled his chair slightly farther from hers, knowing he had to put space between them or she would be in his arms again.

"Let's plan the party. What weekend would be good for you?"

They talked for two more hours, making plans for a barbecue with friends, talking about a variety of subjects, until Grace was exhausted. She moved to her cot, stretching out on the cool sheet. "Wyatt, I have to go to sleep now."

"'Night, Grace," he said, his voice deep.

She lay down and in seconds was asleep. Wyatt sat in the dark, sipping his beer and studying her. She was stretched out on the cot, one arm flung overhead, her skirt hiked higher. Her long legs were smooth and shapely. His gaze ran over her curves and he inhaled deeply. Another sleepless night. He moved to his cot and stretched out, staring at the stars and glancing at the baby who had changed his life forever. He thought about running the ranch, getting someone for the real-estate business in town and in California. In half an hour his thoughts shifted to the party and he began to plan.

Ten o'clock the next morning Grace received a phone call from Wyatt, who was at his office in San Antonio.

"Are you melting?" he asked.

"Actually, we're doing fine. I gave Mrs. Perkins the day off. I hope you don't mind."

"I'm glad you did. It's too hot for her to cook. The earliest I can get someone out there to look at the air conditioner is eleven this morning."

"I'm amazed you've managed that," Grace replied.

"It took bribery, but the guy is a friend of Gabe's and he's coming. I think we'll need a new unit, so it probably means another hot night."

"We'll manage."

"I'm getting the house here aired out and then cooled down. I'll come get you two for dinner and we'll stay here in town tonight. I can't get to the ranch until around four."

"We're doing great. When she had her bath, I let Megan play in the water this morning for a long time and then we went outside where there's a breeze. The crib is still outside in the shade. I'll be careful and see that she doesn't get too hot."

"Sure. The house in town has a pool. Bring your swimsuit."

"Thanks, Mr. Sawyer," Grace replied dryly, trying to remind him of their employer-nanny relationship. "I believe I promised I wouldn't wear anything like a swimsuit around you."

"That was before the air-conditioning broke down. I won't pay any attention to you and even if I do, you won't let it do me any good. Bring your suit and enjoy yourself. Think you can take the heat until four?''

''Yes, Wyatt. Tonight you and Megan should go to your place and I can stay—''

''See you at four. I have to run. We can talk when I see you,'' he said, and broke the connection.

Glaring at the phone, she replaced the receiver. Her pulse skittered at the thought of eating dinner with him and spending the evening with him.

To her surprise, Wyatt was home by half-past three. From the moment he entered the house, she was acutely aware of him. After showering, he changed to a blue, short-sleeved shirt, jeans and his snakeskin boots. He looked incredibly handsome, and she again reminded herself to keep things impersonal and cool between them.

Grace had dressed in one of her plain jumpers and white, short-sleeved blouses, and she had Megan in a pink sundress.

As they drove to town, he talked about his day at work again, about the air conditioner and listened to her tell him every detail about Megan. They ate a long, leisurely dinner in a casual restaurant on the River Walk, and Megan seemed to enjoy the outing as much as the adults. Grace fed her bites from a jar of baby carrots, orange soon dotting the bib tied around Megan's neck.

''It's a small world, Grace,'' Wyatt said, standing and dropping his napkin in his chair.

A couple approached, and a smiling, slightly graying man shook Wyatt's hand. An attractive, older blond woman, dripping with jewelry, gave Wyatt a frosty smile and Grace a cold stare.

''Grace, I'd like you to meet Megan's grandparents, Alexandra and Peter Volmer. This is Grace Talmadge. And there's Megan.''

"Would you like to hold her?" Grace offered, wiping puréed carrots off Megan's chin.

"No, thank you," Alexandra Volmer replied. "I don't believe I want carrots down my front. Another time. She has gotten much bigger. We'll leave you to your date, Mr. Sawyer."

"It's Wyatt, ma'am. I'm Megan's uncle and y'all are her grandparents, so there's no need to be formal."

"It was nice meeting you," Peter Volmer said to Grace, looking one more time at Megan and then nodding at Wyatt before he turned to follow his wife out of the noisy restaurant.

"You should have told them I'm just the nanny. She seemed incredibly cold. How could they not want to hold their granddaughter?"

"Hank said they weren't interested in Megan. I guess he knew what he was talking about," Wyatt said, sitting back down. "I called them the first week I had Megan and told them to come out whenever they wanted to see her."

He gazed after the Volmers and shook his head, then looked at Megan and touched the top of her head lightly. "At least, she doesn't have any idea that she was just rejected. I love you, Meggy," he said, leaning closer to her across the table.

Megan blew a mouthful of carrots at him and he and Grace laughed as she wiped up the carrots. "Good thing you kept your distance there."

"I don't care," Wyatt replied. "I'll wash."

After dinner at dusk, Wyatt drove to a residential area of palatial homes on well-tended lawns. He turned into a wide, circular drive to a sprawling two-story redbrick mansion.

"This is a beautiful home, Wyatt."

"Thanks. My grandfather had it built, and it's been in the Sawyer family ever since."

As soon as they had Megan down for the night, Wyatt gave Grace a tour of the beautifully furnished rooms, with their priceless antiques, gleaming silver and polished hardwood floors, far more elegant than the ranch house. The enormous family room, as well as the dining area and kitchen, all opened onto a long patio. Beyond it was a blue-tile pool with a nearby cabana, lawn chairs and tables and potted plants.

"We can sit in here where it's cool," he said.

"I did bring my swimsuit and since you will be with Megan, I think I'll take this chance to go swim. That pool looks gorgeous and too inviting."

"Sure," he said, nodding.

She smiled at him and hurried out of the room, going upstairs to the bedroom he said was hers for the night. The decor was shades of burgundy and beige with a four-poster bed. Swiftly she changed to a one-piece deep-blue swimsuit, slipped into a terry cover-up, grabbed a towel and left.

The pool was well lit and blue and inviting. She dropped her things on a chair and jumped into the cold water. Her hair was naturally curly, and she didn't worry about getting it wet. She swam laps and then circled leisurely, enjoying herself, when she looked up to see Wyatt seated on the edge of the pool, his bare legs dangling in the water.

Startled, she stared at him. Her mouth went dry and her pulse jumped. He was in a black swimsuit and she could see almost every inch of his sexy, muscled body. She became aware of herself and how little she was wearing, and she didn't want to get out of the water. Less than a foot away, slightly to his right and behind him,

Megan slept peacefully in the baby carrier. Grace had never considered Wyatt's bringing the baby down to the pool. She swam over to him and stood on the pool bottom, water slightly above her waist.

"Want me to take her back upstairs so you can swim?"

"Nope," he said, sliding into the water beside her. He was close, only inches away, his body almost totally bare, and Grace wondered if he could hear her heart pounding.

"We can't both swim and abandon her here by the side of the pool!"

"Wasn't going to," he answered calmly. "You go on with your swim. I'm just cooling off. When you're tired of swimming, if you don't mind, you watch her and I'll swim. There's an intercom on the patio, but I'm not sure we could hear her if we were both swimming and she was upstairs, so I brought her down."

"Good. You swim now. I've already had my turn," she said, and moved closer to the edge of the pool. He stepped in front of her, sliding his arm around her waist.

"Wyatt—"

"It's been a delightful evening, Grace," he said solemnly, and her heart thudded. He pulled her against him as he leaned down to kiss her. His mouth covered hers and his tongue played over hers.

The moment their mouths touched, her insides cartwheeled and an ache started and her breasts tingled. The water was cold, but his body was warm against hers, hard with flat planes and angles. One hand held her head while he kissed her passionately, hot, sweet kisses to create a lifetime of dreams. She knew she should stop him, stop herself, push, move, resist. Instead, she wound her arms around his neck and returned his kisses. She felt his arousal press against her. She wanted to keep kissing, wanted to be in his arms, wanted to toss aside all the resistance to him she'd tried to maintain.

His body felt marvelous. His kisses sent her into a dizzying spiral. There was no way to keep an impersonal relationship between them. Her fingers stroked the strong column of his neck. She shifted closer, pressing her hips against him. When he slipped his bare leg between hers, her heart thudded again. Every touch tore down barriers of resistance, every second of kissing took them headlong into a different relationship.

His hand moved to her breast and his caress shot through her like a lightning bolt. She gasped, too aware, even through the swimsuit, of his hand on her, too conscious of his seductive touch.

She twisted her head. "Wyatt," she whispered.

"Tell me you don't like it, Grace," he whispered in return, bending to kiss her throat while his hand slipped down over her hip and then along the curve of her bottom.

"Want my hand here?" he asked as he stroked her bottom. "Or here?" he whispered while his tongue played in her ear and he caressed her breast again.

She caught his hand. With all the effort she could summon, she opened her eyes to look at him. "Stop now, Wyatt. We had agreements about these things."

"I don't remember any agreement that I wouldn't kiss you," he said, nuzzling her throat.

She moaned softly, but she pushed against him and slipped out of his arms. "You have to stop."

He gazed at her and reached out to place his palm against her cheek. "I'll stop for now." He turned and swam away.

The moment he put distance between them, she

jumped up on the side of the pool to sit, her legs dangling in the water.

Wyatt turned to watch her and then swam over to her, catching her ankles in his hands, caressing her ankles and calves lightly. "I didn't want to ruin your swim. If you'll wait, I'll be just a few minutes and then I'll stay with Megan."

"Swim all you want. I don't mind," she said, too aware of his hands on her ankles and legs, of Wyatt so close, even though he was in the pool and she was out. Too aware of her wet swimsuit and all the exposed skin.

He smiled and swam away. Her heart was still pounding and her lips and her body still tingled. Desire was hot and intense. She should quit this job, but where would she find another job that would pay like this one? She looked at the sleeping baby and knew she was beginning to love Megan as if she were her own.

She touched Megan's soft curls. "You'll both break my heart, just like Virginia said." While Wyatt's powerful arms cut through the water, she remembered exactly how it had felt to be pressed against him, to have his bare leg between her legs. Handsome, sexy, charming, intelligent. It wasn't fair to have all that rolled up in one six-foot-four-inch package.

He climbed out at the deep end, walked away and then turned to run and dive into the pool. She shook her head, knowing even if it was his own pool, it wasn't safe to run on wet tiles. Did he always have to do something risky? And break rules? She suspected she was merely another challenge to him. Why else would he be interested in her?

Then he was splashing up out of the water in front of her. He jumped up to sit beside her on the edge of the pool. "I'm through. You can swim now."

"I'm going to bed," she said quietly, suspecting if she stayed, Wyatt would also stay.

"Okay, we'll all go in," he said cheerfully.

She stood, crossing to the chair to get her cover-up and slip it on. She turned to find Wyatt watching her. His dark gaze burned with blatant desire and she inhaled swiftly, her insides heating. She belted the cover-up and picked up her towel. "Good night, Wyatt."

He got to his feet, picked up the carrier and fell into step beside her. "I'm coming, too." As he held open the door, he said, "I've been thinking about this party we'll have—"

"Not we, Wyatt. You. Do I have to keep reminding you I'm only the nanny?"

"Right, Grace. Anyway, I think I'll ask Ashley Brant to help me with a guest list, because I don't know who lives here any longer and who doesn't, and who I should ask and who I shouldn't."

"I don't know who Ashley Brant is."

"She's Gabe's wife and her family lives on Cotton Creek. She went to school in Stallion Pass, so she has the same background Gabe and Josh and I do."

"Then she sounds like a good one to ask about a guest list."

As they walked down the hall, Grace asked, "Where did the name Stallion Pass come from?"

"It's an old legend. There was an Apache warrior who fell in love with a cavalryman's daughter. The cavalry killed the warrior, and according to legend, his ghost returned as a white stallion that roams this area. That's where the name originated. According to the story, whoever tames the stallion finds his true love."

"That's sad and romantic."

"What fuels the legend is that there have been wild, white stallions in these parts for years."

"Anyone try to catch and tame one?"

"Not that I know of. Guess no one wanted true love to come that badly," he said, and she laughed. "Want a glass of wine or cold lemonade before we turn in?" he asked.

"You're wearing me down, Wyatt. Yes, thanks. I'll take the lemonade."

He smiled. "Good." They entered the kitchen and Wyatt crossed the room. Wyatt had his towel around his neck; otherwise, the only clothing he wore was his swimsuit, and she was intensely conscious of him. Clothing was a slim barrier between them, but nonetheless, it was a barrier, and she hoped her long skirts and high-necked blouses cooled Wyatt's interest in her, but she knew her swimsuit wouldn't.

"Wyatt, I'll go change and put Megan into her crib. You know, I really shouldn't have accepted the glass of lemonade."

He crossed the room to her and touched her chin lightly. "Don't go all proper on me. I'll keep my distance. Just come back down and talk to me," he said, smiling at her.

"Wyatt, you're hopeless. I'm struggling to keep everything between us as impersonal as possible. This is a game to you."

"No, it's no game," he said solemnly. "And impersonal flew away back there in that first interview when you asked me about my experience as a daddy. Come on. Relax. I won't bite."

She felt ridiculous protesting when he was being easygoing and charming, yet she knew she was right. "All right, but I'm putting on my jeans and a T-shirt."

He grinned. "Scared I might peel you right out of that suit? Or does it disturb you to see me in a swimsuit?"

She knew he was teasing, and she laughed. "You like trouble, don't you, Wyatt."

"It's all I know."

"I don't believe that, and you'll have to be good for Megan's sake."

"You're right there, but I don't have to be good with you. You need a bad boy in your life, Grace."

"No, I don't."

"Someday I'll get Jett to come up to the house and stay with Megan and I'll get you to ride on my hog with me."

"I don't think so."

He stepped closer, his arm slipping inside Grace's cover-up and circling her waist to pull her close.

Seven

"When you come back, you'll be covered up from chin to toe. Give me one more kiss while we're both half-naked, Grace," he whispered, pushing open the cover-up and pressing against her as he kissed her.

She didn't fight him this time, but wound her arms around his neck and kissed him in return, responding fully, feeling his arousal, too aware of their almost naked bodies pressed together.

He kissed her senseless. She lost awareness of their surroundings, of time, of everything except Wyatt and his hard body. When he released her, she opened her eyes to find him watching her.

His breathing was as ragged as hers and she stared at him, wanting to pull him back and kiss him more, but reason was swiftly returning and she knew she should be glad he stopped.

"We may be drawn to each other, Wyatt, but it doesn't

mean anything. *That* I'm sure you can understand. I'll see you shortly.'' She picked up the carrier with Megan and left without looking back. As soon as she had the baby in her crib and was in her own bedroom, Grace closed her eyes. One lie on top of another. Where had her impeccable honesty gone? His kisses didn't mean anything—to him. To her, they meant everything. His kisses changed their relationship, changed how she saw him, changed how she felt, changed her job and her life. Could she ever forget Wyatt?

Could she possibly be falling in love with him? She hadn't been with him a month yet and he was storming her senses, demolishing her defenses. She would call that Ashley Brant and ask her to make sure there were some beautiful single women on the party-invitation list so Wyatt could meet them or renew old friendships.

She walked to the mirror and stared at herself. Her lips were swollen from his kisses, her wet hair plastered to her head.

''Drink one glass of lemonade and go. Don't let him near you,'' she told her reflection. She hadn't worked for him very long and already their nanny-employer relationship was in shambles. At least she thought it was in shambles. Wyatt probably thought the situation was improving.

''Resist.''

She showered, dried her hair, dressed in jeans and a T-shirt. She went downstairs where she kept a distance between them and kept the conversation only on plans for a party. After one glass of lemonade, she went back to her room. He had looked amused at her abrupt departure, but had let her go without touching her again.

He, too, had changed into a T-shirt and jeans. He switched off lights and went out by the pool to sit on a chaise, putting his bare feet up. It was three in the morning now, and lights sparkled on the water, but all he saw was Grace and how she'd looked tonight at the pool. She was gorgeous, and he had wanted to take off her swimsuit that clung so revealingly to every curve.

Just remembering took his breath and made him hard with desire. He wanted her more than he could remember ever wanting a woman. And he liked being with her more than with any woman he had ever known. When he was at work, he was beginning to look forward to getting home and seeing her again.

This constant eagerness to see her and be with her, even just to talk, was proof that it wasn't just the challenge she presented that drew him. She was wonderful with Megan, managed everything about the house, and Mrs. Perkins liked her enormously.

He had been in love too many times to count in his life, and he knew he was drawn to Grace now. Love, excitement, touching, physical relationships, shared times—he liked them all, but he wanted his freedom to do as he pleased. Yet the thought of marrying Grace sent a ripple of excitement through him. Marriage to Grace. Was that so improbable? It would be good for Megan.

Marriage to Grace. He would have to think about that one.

Wyatt shifted, staring at the water and lost in thoughts about Grace. He wanted her in his arms, in his bed, in his life. The realization surprised him, and he knew he needed to know her better, to get to know his own feelings better.

He sighed. Between Megan and Grace he hadn't had a whole night's sleep in weeks. And he didn't see any improvement looming in the future.

* * *

The next day a new air conditioner was installed, and Grace hoped their lives would get back on track and she would see little of Wyatt. That afternoon she was in the ranch yard swinging Megan in the baby swing when a pickup drove up. Wyatt emerged from the house and strode across the yard toward it.

Josh Kellogg climbed out of the truck and waved at her. Just as she waved back, Wyatt reached Josh and the two men faced each other. She was too far away to hear what they were saying, but she could see that Wyatt's friend was angry with him.

Wyatt could see the fire in Josh's eyes. Josh's fists were clenched, and Wyatt was ready to duck in case one of those fists came swinging.

"You go into town and talk to the bank," Josh was saying. "Dammit to hell, Wyatt, I know you meant well, but you can't pay off my loan for me. It's my problem, not yours."

"I didn't do it for you, so just calm down."

"The hell you didn't. You don't know Laurie, and if this is because we agreed to be Megan's guardians if something happened to you, you get Gabe and Ashley for guardians. You're not paying off my loan."

"I did it for your dad," Wyatt said quietly. He yanked off his shirt and turned around. "Remember this, Josh?"

He turned back to face his friend. "Your dad stopped those terrible beatings."

Josh gaze into the distance, a frustrated, angry scowl on his face. "Okay, I guess you're grateful for that, but that was my dad, not me. I didn't have anything to do with it. The damn bank won't redo the loan. As far as they're concerned, this is between you and me."

"I want to do this because of your dad. The money

means nothing. Do you want to see my bank books and savings and see how much I'm worth? I'll never miss the money, Josh. Never. And money by itself means nothing if you can't do what you want with it. And it wasn't just your dad. If it hadn't been for you having me over at your place so much, I wouldn't have known your dad. You two let me live on your ranch for months on end. Do you have any idea what that meant to me at that time in my life?"

"Wyatt, it just doesn't seem right."

"Did it seem right for you two to give me a home when we were kids?"

"Of course it did. That's entirely different."

"It was another mouth to feed. You did plenty for me back then. Now let me do this for you. I'm serious, Josh. I'll never miss the money. I had more money than my dad even before I came back here."

Josh's brows arched. "You made that much in California?"

"Yes, I did, and if it makes you feel better, you can look at my financial statements or you can talk to my California accountant. I think you can guess what the Texas inheritance is worth."

Josh stared at him in silence.

"Come on, Josh, let me do this. I'm just sorry I didn't do something when your dad was alive."

"Oh, hell. You always could talk your way into or out of anything. I'll feel like I owe you my life. But you're not getting my wife or my firstborn."

Wyatt relaxed and grinned, reaching out to clasp his friend on the shoulder. "That's fine."

"You're something else, Wyatt."

"Now do me a favor and keep this quiet. It's just between our two families. I don't want word out in town that I've turned rich and charitable.''

Josh laughed. ''All right. And you know my mare, Gladiola. Well, you can have her foal, her firstborn. That foal is going to be one great horse.''

''I might take you up on that.''

''Thanks,'' Josh said, offering his hand. His eyes sparkled. ''Now that we've got that out of the way, I can tell you my news. Laurie and I are expecting our first child.''

''Congratulations! That's great.'' Wyatt pumped his friend's hand.

''I'd like to see Megan now,'' Josh said. ''You know, I'm going to owe you my soul.''

Wyatt laughed as the two turned toward the yard. ''No, you're not. Consider it a gift to your dad, not to you. It's for days long gone, but they saved me from some hellish moments.''

''I'm glad. My dad wasn't very responsible when it came to running the ranch or making money, but he was a good man and a good dad.''

''He gave me hope.''

''Hey, Wyatt, I'll tell you what—I'll throw in another gift. Gabe caught a wild white stallion that has been running in these parts. He had gotten in with some of Quinn Ryder's good mares and bred them, and Quinn wanted him caught. Gabe couldn't tame him and gave him to me. I can't do anything with him. He's yours if you want him.''

''Sure. I'll take him.''

''You're not scared of the legend?'' Josh asked, grinning.

''Hardly.''

''Well, remember, Gabe had the stallion and now

Gabe's married. I have the stallion now and I'm married.''

''No danger. Give me that wild horse and I'll tame him and I *won't* end up married. It'll be interesting.''

''He's yours. You were warned.''

''I don't believe that legend and you don't, either.'' They reached the back gate and walked through it to join Grace and Megan who were on a blanket on the grass. A slight breeze cooled the air and the spreading branches of a tall oak shaded the area.

''Hi,'' Josh said to Grace as they approached. She smiled when he caught the swing and bent down to talk to Megan.

Then he straightened. ''We'll have you over for supper soon, Wyatt. You bring Megan and you can look at my prize mare.'' He turned to Grace. ''You come along, too, Grace. Laurie would love to talk to you about Megan, I'm sure.''

''Thanks, Josh. We'll do that,'' Wyatt answered easily.

''I better get home.''

He turned away and Wyatt walked with him back to his pickup. After he drove away, Wyatt returned to sit down beside Megan.

''I'm glad Josh seemed so happy when he left,'' Grace said. ''He looked angry when he first arrived.''

''He had a bee in his bonnet over ranch stuff, but it's all smoothed out. They're going to have their first child.''

''Ah,'' Grace said. ''I wondered why his wife would want to talk to me. We've never met.''

''You'll know her when you see her. She's a gorgeous woman, a model, and does a lot of commercials for this area. She probably wants to ask you questions about baby care.''

Grace laughed. ''So now I'm an expert.''

"You're getting to be one. You'll meet her at our party."

"*Your* party, Wyatt. Not ours."

"It was your idea. You're helping me plan it. You'll be my hostess, so that makes it our party."

"Do you ever lose arguments?"

"Yep. About eighty percent of the time with you," Wyatt replied, touching the tip of her nose lightly. "Josh is giving me a wild, white stallion. Gabe caught the horse and couldn't tame him and gave him to Josh who doesn't want him."

"Is it tame now?"

"Not at all."

"And you want the challenge of taming him?" she asked.

"Yep. Josh wanted to know if I was scared of the old legend."

"That's ridiculous," she remarked, gazing into Wyatt's inscrutable dark eyes. "You won't fall in love because you own a horse."

"I don't think so, either," he said.

Megan began to fuss, and Grace picked her up. "Come here, sweetie."

"I better head to town. See you tonight." He leaned over to kiss Megan. "Bye, bye, darlin'."

"Say goodbye to Daddy," Grace said, waving the baby's hand.

Wyatt looked at her sharply. "Daddy?" he asked.

"I've been meaning to ask you—do you want her to call you Uncle Wyatt or Daddy? You'll be Daddy to her. You already are. Your brother Hank wouldn't object, would he?"

"No, he wouldn't. I'll tell her about her real mother

and daddy when she's old enough to understand, but, yes, I'd like it if she called me Daddy.''

"That makes sense to me. So Daddy it is. That's what I've been saying to her, anyway.''

"One more decision out of my hands," he said dryly. "Bye, sweet stuff," he said, brushing Megan's cheek with another kiss. Bye, Nanny," he added, and brushed Grace's cheek with a quick kiss, too.

"Wyatt, if Mrs. Perkins sees you, there'll be wild rumors all over this ranch.''

"I'm trying to reform, but there are moments when it isn't going to happen." He stood and was gone, striding toward the garage. He usually left in the sports car, but today he got on his motorcycle, waved at her and then with a roar and stirring up of dust, he sped out of sight.

For the next week he was gone during the day, but he spent every evening with Grace and Megan until Friday night after supper. Grace was in the family room with Megan when Wyatt appeared at the door. He had changed to a T-shirt and Jeans. "Josh is bringing the stallion over now," he announced. "Want to bring Megan and see the new horse?"

"Yes, I do," Grace said, picking up Megan.

It was a warm summer evening and while they waited for Josh to arrive, they sat on the porch. Wyatt held Megan, playing with her until Josh drove into view, pulling a horse trailer behind his pickup.

They all went to the corral where Wyatt opened the gate for Josh to drive inside. Standing outside the corral, Grace watched the muscles ripple in Wyatt's back and arms as he worked and her throat went dry. Sexy man. Just the sight of him could make her heart race.

Wyatt waited while Josh drove inside and then he entered the corral and closed the gate behind them.

A terrible racket shook the horse trailer, and Grace realized the stallion was kicking and fighting to get out. When he whinnied loudly, she drew a deep breath, watching both men who acted as if nothing unusual was happening.

"I'll let him out," Wyatt said. "You stay in the pickup."

Josh nodded and waited. Wyatt opened the trailer and the animal burst out, whirling to run.

Wyatt slammed shut the trailer and then ran to the gate. While Josh drove out, the horse reached the fence. He reared, whinnying loudly and then turned to run again. He bucked and reared and Grace thought he was a fearful sight, but she noticed Wyatt and Josh seemed to pay little attention to him.

"Thanks, Josh," Wyatt said.

"I don't think you're getting any prize. He's too wild for me."

Wyatt glanced at the stallion. "We'll see. It'll give me something to do in my spare moments. Come up to the house and have a cold drink with us."

"Sure, thanks."

They all went to the porch where Wyatt once again took Megan and Josh held her for a few minutes. Grace enjoyed sitting and listening to the two friends talk about old times and their ranches. Wyatt was charming, relaxed and constantly attentive to Megan until she began to fuss, and Grace knew Megan was growing sleepy.

"I'll take her to bed," Grace said, taking the baby from Wyatt, conscious of her hands brushing his.

When she returned, they sat on the darkened porch for another hour before Josh left for home.

Then, as they had done every night as soon as Megan was asleep, Wyatt discussed the upcoming party with Grace.

Later that night when she couldn't sleep and went to the window, she could see lights at the corral and Wyatt moving around inside with the wild stallion. One more wild thing that he was involved with.

Ashley Brant had helped with the guest list for the party, and the Saturday night of the barbecue, the last of June, finally arrived. It was a blessedly cool night, so they could enjoy the patio and yard, as well as the inside of the house.

Before the guests arrived, Grace dressed Megan in a frilly pink dress, a pink hair bow, lace-trimmed pink socks and tiny white sandals.

"Let's go show you to Daddy," Grace said. "C'mon, sweetie." She picked up Megan and went to the family room and then to the dining room to find Wyatt. He was having the dinner catered, and men and women in uniforms moved through the house, setting up the food and bar.

"Wyatt."

He turned and Grace's heart missed a beat. He was dressed casually, yet he looked incredibly handsome in jeans, a plaid, short-sleeved shirt and snakeskin boots.

"Hi, sweet baby," he said, crossing the room to take Megan. "She looks adorable."

"Yes, she does."

He stared at Grace's outfit, which was frumpy to the extreme—plain brown dress of the kind of fabric that looked better suited for flour sacking. It was loosely belted over a thick waist.

He poked her middle. "What the hell, Grace?"

"It's padding, but I think it'll prevent any rumors about us being an item."

"I'm not worried about rumors. You don't need to come to this party looking like someone's elderly aunt." He reached out to remove a pair of ugly black-framed glasses from her nose.

"No, this is better, Wyatt. Think about Megan. You told me a long time ago that because of Megan, you didn't want a whisper of scandal connected to you now."

He studied Grace's hair, which was slicked back in a bun behind her head. No tendrils escaped. With the padding, glasses, old-lady shoes and flour-sack dress, she wouldn't get a second glance.

"There'll be a few nice single guys here tonight. Sure you want to meet them looking like that?" he asked dryly, thinking it suited him fine if his single friends didn't give her a second glance.

"I think I remember you saying something about no boyfriends out here, so it's just as well I don't meet anyone I want to start dating. Right?"

He handed her the glasses and watched her put them back on. "I don't know—at a glance, you're right. No rumors, but if you get up close and talk to anyone, I think they'll be able to see past the glasses and dress and all."

"You didn't that first day."

He laughed. "All right. Wear your fake glasses and sit in the corner and be obscure. You'll be missing all the fun at the party. You'll see."

The doorbell rang and he left her, carrying Megan away with him, and from the arrival of the first guests, he was busy. Grace faded into a corner and watched, seeing Wyatt at his most charming. Once he entered the room with a beautiful woman beside him, and he shot

Grace an angry glance before he turned to introduce the woman to other guests.

Grace could guess the reason for the annoyed look, and in minutes, her guess was confirmed when Wyatt came over to her to hand Megan to her. "I think she needs changing. Grace, I thought I took all these single women off the guest list."

"I dug the list out of the trash and put them back on," she said sweetly as she took the baby from him. "You need to meet some women you can date. You won't be so lonesome and bored out here."

"Grace, I get about three calls a day from single women. They bring me casseroles to the office. They ask me out. That's one reason I don't want to live in town. Now, dammit, I don't want to encourage any—"

"Wyatt, just get to know them. You might have a lot of entertainment, and you need the diversion in your life. And then you wouldn't simply hit on the nearest available female." Grace smiled and left before he could reply.

As she walked away, Wyatt swore under his breath.

"Wyatt, your home is beautiful," a tall, slender blonde said, slipping her arm through his. He turned, trying to smile, yet wanting to follow his nanny and give her a lecture about interfering in his life and reminding her that he hadn't hit on her simply because she was the nearest available female.

Kids ran through the house, and it was filled with his neighbors, old friends, people who hadn't spoken to him that last summer he'd been at home, but who seemed to be enjoying his hospitality now.

Later in the evening he was standing with his best friends looking at Gabe and Ashley's two children as they moved about the room. Five-year-old Julian was carrying his eleven-month-old baby sister. "I can't believe how your kids have grown," Wyatt said.

"Ella makes Julian look all grown up. He's not such a little boy any longer," Gabe Brant said.

"Wyatt, does Grace Talmadge work all week for you?" Ashley asked. "Does she have any free days?"

"She's off on weekends."

"She's wonderful with children," Ashley said. "I was hoping she had some days when we could hire her for Julian and Ella. We lost our nanny when she graduated from college." They stood watching Grace, who was at one of the long tables in the dining room. Five small children were clustered around her, and she was assisting each of them to get second helpings of food.

"Sorry, but I've got her full-time."

"If she ever quits, please let us know," Ashley said. "And she's so considerate of you. She asked me to put some extra single women on the guest list."

Gabe grinned at his wife. "Why? Does she think Wyatt needs help meeting women? That'll be the day."

"I think she just thought he'd been away so long and was a little isolated out here on the ranch—"

Gabe and Josh both laughed. "Isolated—Wyatt?" Gabe said, and Ashley laughed.

"I didn't stop to think. I suppose you're right," Ashley admitted.

"Who are you dating, Wyatt?" Gabe asked. "Anyone here?"

"Nope. I've been dating a woman in California."

"You should have brought her out here for this party," Gabe said.

"I'm sorry, Wyatt," Ashley said. "Although I see you did invite the women I had on the list."

"Grace did that. I scratched their names off."

"You're lucky to have her," Ashley said.

"I am lucky," Wyatt answered, watching Grace. He shifted Megan in his arms, barely aware of his friends' conversation as he thought about Grace. In minutes everyone moved away except Josh, who studied Wyatt.

"I don't think you're about to let your nanny hire out to someone else even if she wasn't full-time here."

"Why do you think that?" Wyatt asked. He looked at Josh and saw the sparkle in his eyes.

"I saw her the last time I was here. I don't remember any glasses and I seemed to remember she had a more appealing shape."

"You're damned observant."

"And what the two of you do is your own business. I'm not prying, but I think there's one good-looking nanny under that disguise."

"I hope you're the only person here tonight who knows that. I'm trying to avoid the sort of scandal that's always followed me. I don't want more scandal in Megan's life."

"I'd guess I'm the only person who's noticed the disguise. Gabe hasn't. But then, he's never seen her before. No, tonight I don't think anyone would look twice. And Megan, too, lends you an air of respectability. Ah. Here comes Gretchen, one of those women your nanny thought you should invite. I'm getting out of the way now, because I know Gretchen wants to talk to you, not me."

"You stay right here."

"Nah. I've been away from my wife too long. She's over there talking to her dad, and I haven't gotten to say hello to him tonight."

"Did I run Josh away?" Gretchen said, gazing up at Wyatt. She was a brunette with big blue eyes and a lush figure, yet Wyatt just wanted to escape.

"No, of course not. Gretchen, would you excuse me? I need to change Megan."

"I think it's the sweetest thing the way you've become such a caring parent. Let me go with you and see the nursery. This house is just beautiful."

Wyatt barely heard her. He didn't know whether Megan needed changing or not, but as an escape ploy, it had failed. As he crossed the room, Gretchen at his side, Grace glanced at him. He gave her a meaningful look, wanting to shake her for inviting all these single females.

She smiled sweetly at him and then bent over a child's plate. He sighed and tried to listen to Gretchen.

Three hours later he stood on the front drive and waved goodbye to the last of the departing guests. He walked back inside to find Megan tidying up the few things the caterers had left undone.

"Don't clean," he said, catching her hand. "Let's sit on the back porch and have a drink and relax. We can hear Megan over the intercom if she cries."

In minutes they were on the porch and he had pulled off his boots and unbuttoned his shirt. Grace had been to her room to change to cutoffs and a T-shirt, and she sat beside him.

"It was a very nice party, Wyatt."

"It was a good idea, so thanks. You're right. I need to do things so Megan will have friends."

"She'll have friends when she goes to school and gets into activities, but it's good for you to get to know people now."

"I'm not even going to think about those women you invited—you did me no favors there. Don't you know I can find someone to date on my own?" he said, setting down his bottle of beer and turning his chair to face hers.

He reached for her and pulled her onto his lap. "I've wanted to do this all evening."

"Wyatt!"

"I want you, Grace. And having all those women around here tonight just made me more aware of how much I want you and you alone."

"Wyatt, stop. I'm not your kind of woman. We have nothing in common. You've never dated anyone like me, have you? Someone quiet and bookish. You don't even like to read. You drive too fast, you fly your own plane—"

"You talk too much," he said, and kissed her.

Grace wanted to resist, but it was impossible. Wyatt could melt her resistance with the stroke of his tongue. He leaned away. "I'm going to Houston Tuesday," he said. "I'm flying down. Come with me for the day."

"No. Surely you don't want to take Megan on a plane!"

"Megan will be fine. If there's any bad weather, we won't go. It'll be interesting. C'mon, Grace, live a little. I promise I'll get you both there in one piece."

She put her fingers on his mouth. "Don't make promises like that. You can't control life."

"I sure as hell can't control you. Come with me, please," he whispered, showering kisses on her throat and ear. "Go with me, Grace. Stop living in a bubble."

"Some bubble," she whispered. "All right, Wyatt. You win. I'll go. I'll be terrified of flying in a little plane, but I'll go."

Tuesday morning Wyatt fastened Megan into her carrier in the back seat of his pickup. As soon as he and Grace were buckled in, they drove away. It was a gorgeous day, deep-blue skies, a slight breeze and bright sunshine, and Grace bubbled with anticipation at spending part of the day with Wyatt.

She glanced at him swiftly, taking in his jeans, white shirt and black boots. He had a sports coat with him, which he would probably wear to his appointment. She smoothed her navy skirt, thinking most people would still give her little notice.

"I reserved a hotel room so you'll have a place to relax while I take care of business. It's in a good shopping area, too."

"Thank you," she said. "Megan loves to go out—she must get that from her uncle—so she'll be happy."

As they left the ranch, Grace turned to him. "I thought you said you have your own runway and hangar on the ranch."

"I do, but I need to see Ashley Brant this morning."

"Your friends are wonderful. And Ashley seems to adore Megan."

At Gabe's they slowed at the back gate. Ashley and Julian came out of the house and approached the truck. Then Quinn Ryder, Ashley's father, stepped out of the house with Ella in his arms. "Here comes the family to greet us," Wyatt said. He got out and reached back in to unbuckle Megan and pick her up.

"Are we going in?" Grace asked, and he grinned.

"I have a surprise. Ashley's keeping Megan for me so you and I can have a day in the city on our own."

Eight

"**W**yatt Sawyer, you didn't tell me that!"

He grabbed Megan's bag and shut the pickup door, leaving Grace sputtering. She climbed out just as Ashley and Julian arrived, both of them smiling at her.

"Hi, Grace," Ashley said. "I'm looking forward to watching Megan today. Laurie is coming over to learn a few things about babies. Although Megan and Ella aren't tiny babies any longer."

"Ashley," Grace said, "I only just found out that Megan would be staying with you. I'm—"

"It's a surprise," Wyatt interjected easily. "I thought my nanny needed a day of relaxation, and Grace hasn't been to Houston in a long time, have you?"

She gave him a stormy look and stood with her hands on her hips.

"Well, enjoy yourself while Wyatt works," Ashley

said. "And don't worry about Megan. I'll take good care of her."

"We'll all take good care of her," Quinn Ryder said, smiling at Grace, and she had to smile in return.

In minutes she was back in the pickup with Wyatt, waving at everyone as they turned and drove away.

She faced Wyatt. "Of all the deceitful, low-down tricks—"

"No worse than you asking all those single females to our party without telling me," he said, reaching for her hand. "Stop getting your feathers in a fluff over a day in town. Relax and enjoy it. I'll be working and you can do as you please."

"Wyatt, men don't take their nannies off on plane trips without the baby just to be nice."

"This man does."

"Well, that will not be how the Brants and Mr. Ryder will see it."

"So how will they see it?" Wyatt asked.

"You know darn good and well they'll think we're going off to spend the day in bed."

"Now there's a thought!"

"Wyatt!"

He laughed. "Don't be ridiculous. We can spend the day in bed at my house, if that's what's going on. No, they'll think we're going to do just what I told them. I said you'd do some shopping."

She threw up her hands. "I still think it was sneaky to not tell me."

"Was it sneaky for you to avoid telling me about fishing that guest list out of the trash and inviting all the women I had scratched off the list?"

"All right. We're even."

"So smile."

She looked at him and laughed. "Wyatt, you're something else."

"Nope. I'm just a guy wanting to have a good day."

And soon she was buckled into the private jet beside Wyatt and on the way to Houston. Once there, they drove first to the hotel and he went up to the room with her. She gave him a look as he unlocked the door and motioned her inside ahead of him.

"You're coming in?" she asked. "I thought you had business."

"I do. I have an appointment in thirty minutes and I'll be on time. I'm just coming in for a few minutes so we can make plans."

She walked into a large suite that overlooked the patio and pool area. She crossed the room to look below and then turned to face Wyatt, who was poking through the briefcase he carried. He set it down and faced her.

"Here's where I'll be if you need me," he said. "Here's my cell phone."

"I won't need you and I'm not calling you while you're engaged in business."

"Suits me if you do. I'll be through about three today. We can go out for an early dinner tonight and then head home."

She planted her hands on her hips. "What other surprises have you got, Wyatt? Do you have this hotel room for the night?"

"No, I don't. You heard me tell Ashley that we'd see her tonight."

"So when do we check out of here?"

"I asked if we could keep the room until four. We'll go to dinner—no one knows us here so no rumors will start—then we'll fly home. Now, does that meet with your approval?"

"Yes. I don't know why you bother asking. If it didn't, you'd talk me into it."

"I do have something I want to talk you into."

"Oh, brother, here it comes," she said, narrowing her eyes.

He smiled and took her purse to open it and slide a card inside. "Here's a credit card of mine. This isn't a bribe. There are no strings attached." He put her purse in the chair. "Go shopping today. I don't see any reason for you to work in those awful dresses you wear. I'm going to notice you whether you do or you don't, so why don't you come into this century and get some other clothes? Buy something to wear to dinner tonight."

"Wyatt, I'm not going to become your sleep-in nanny. You're irresistible to women and you know it, but I will not move into your bed. We've kissed and I knew we shouldn't have, because look what it's led to—this."

"You sound like I'm asking you to jump out of the hotel window this afternoon. Just buy some cute clothes, something besides that schoolmarm stuff to go out in tonight."

"Thanks, Wyatt. You're very generous, but you've been running around with women who've warped your view of life. They are entirely different from me. He stepped closer and she glanced at her watch. "Don't you have to be somewhere now?"

"I'm not late, but I need to go." He reached into his pocket. "Here's a list of nice shops where I have accounts—they know you might be in today. Get whatever you want. I'm going to make some money this afternoon and you can spend some."

"How long have you been planning this?"

"For about a week. Didn't you enjoy the flight this morning?"

"Yes, I did. You were right about that, but you're still not getting me into your bed with all this, even if your kisses *are* irresistible."

"I didn't know for sure they were irresistible," he said quietly, dropping his briefcase and closing the distance between them. "If that's the case, kiss me goodbye." He wrapped his arms around her and leaned down to kiss her, smothering her protest and kissing her until she clung to him and kissed him back.

When he stopped, she opened her eyes and stared at him.

"And you *will* be in my bed," he said in a husky voice. "I want you." He picked up his briefcase and strode to the door. He glanced over his shoulder at her. "See you at four. Go buy a pretty dress and some pretty dresses to work in. Something that doesn't cover you from chin to ankles."

Annoyed beyond measure with both herself and him, she snatched up a small vase on a nearby table and threw it at the closing door. The door shut and the vase struck it, shattering into pieces.

Appalled at her loss of temper, Grace stared at the bits of glass, unable to believe what she'd done. She couldn't recall losing control like that ever before. Not with her sisters or anyone. Suddenly the door opened and he thrust his head inside, looked down at the smashed vase and then at her.

"Wow! I didn't know you'd do something like that. They'll just put it on the bill. Let them clean it up, too. So it seems you can let go when you want to, darlin'," he said, chuckling as he closed the door.

"Tarnation, Wyatt Sawyer," she said, glaring at the closed door. Contrary to his suggestion, she crossed to it to kneel and pick up the broken pieces of china. Then she moved restlessly around the hotel room, looking outside at the beautiful day. At last she picked up her purse. He wanted her to go shopping. Okay, that was what she would do. But she wasn't going to climb into bed with him. She wasn't going to be a live-in nanny, as well as a live-in lover. She just hoped she had sense enough to stop letting him kiss her and to stop kissing him back.

She thought about Megan. She missed her. She'd never told Wyatt, but when she left on weekends, she missed Megan. She'd given up her apartment in San Antonio to save money, so on weekends she stayed in a cheap hotel or with friends. Weekends were usually long, sometimes lonely, and she missed Megan dreadfully. She hated to admit it, but she missed Wyatt, too.

Grace pulled out the list of shops, squared her shoulders and left the hotel.

She spent most of the day buying clothes, but she also went to a bookstore to get herself three new books and one for Wyatt. She spent her own money for the books. He might pitch his book into the trash, but there was a chance he'd read it. She returned to the hotel by two and showered, getting ready for her early dinner date with Wyatt.

"All right, Wyatt Sawyer, you want me to wear something that isn't schoolmarmish," she told her reflection in the full-length mirror.

She had bought black lace underwear, which she stepped into. Then she pulled on a black dinner dress. It was clinging, short enough to stop inches above her knees and had a soft drape around the neckline to plunge to her waist in back. She piled her hair on her head loosely, letting curls fall around her face. Finally she stepped into high-heeled black sandals. She studied herself as she put on makeup.

She twisted and turned and didn't see how he could call this dress schoolmarmish. She bought a small black envelope purse. Glancing at her watch, she saw he was ten minutes late and she wondered what he was doing.

She'd had his book gift-wrapped, and now as she stared at it, she suspected he would be disappointed. She had bought him a box of chocolates, too, and those she knew he would like.

Wyatt knocked before he unlocked the door and stepped inside. He was late, tired of dealing with business and eager to see Grace. "Hi, darlin', I'm home," he called, remembering how Grace had tossed a vase at the door.

All evidence of it was gone now, the carpet swept clean.

Grace strolled through the door from the bedroom, and he sucked in his breath at the sight of her. He'd known from that first night that she was gorgeous, but most of the time, she kept that beauty hidden. Not tonight. He stared and his temperature spiked up twenty degrees. He wanted to stay right here in the hotel room and take her out of the fantastic black dress.

She had done what he wanted beyond his wildest dreams. The dress molded her full curves, revealed long, luscious legs and her slender arms and throat.

"You look beautiful," he said, moving toward her. "You take my breath away."

"You approve of the dress?" she asked, turning for him. When he saw the plunging back, he wondered if she wore anything beneath the slip of a dress. The dark hose and pumps showed off her legs.

"I more than approve."

"Thank you. I bought you a present—with my own

money,'' she said, smiling at him and picking up a small sack.

It was an effort to stop staring at her. He knew she had tried to get something to please him, but all he wanted to do was look at her and touch her. He took the sack, sat in the nearest chair and caught her wrist to pull her down on his lap. ''Come here while I open my present.''

She sat perched on his knees while he opened the sack and ripped wrapping paper off a box of chocolates. ''Yum,'' he said, looking at her mouth. ''Thank you.'' He opened his other present and pulled out a book entitled *History of the Lone Star State*.

''I know you don't read much, but I thought you might enjoy parts of this about the time when your great-great-grandfather settled in Texas. I've read it before, and it's a particularly interesting book.''

''If you gave it to me, I will love it.'' His arm tightened around her waist, but she slipped off his lap quickly and stood.

''Now are you taking me to dinner?''

Amused, he gazed up at her. He wanted to pull her back into his arms and kiss away all her protests and seduce her. But he would stick to his plans for the evening and take her to dinner and dancing. He wondered if she even danced. He'd find out soon enough.

''Yes, we'll go to dinner. Let's get your things. I've already checked out of the hotel.''

''I'll pay for the vase, Wyatt.''

He grinned. ''No. I wouldn't have missed that for the world. I didn't know you ever let go like that.''

''I don't. You drove me to losing my temper, but it's not going to happen again.''

He grinned and touched her cheek. "Want to make a little wager?"

"No! I don't bet. And never with you. Now, let's not get into another hassle because I've had a wonderful day and I'm looking forward to dinner. I skipped lunch."

"Why did you do that?"

"I was busy shopping. I spent two hours in the bookstore."

"Two hours with books?"

"You should try reading. Books are wonderful."

"Grace, I didn't finish high school."

"That doesn't have a thing to do with reading. One of my grandfathers didn't finish high school, yet he read constantly, and he read to me and my sisters when we were little. I think he's why I like to read."

"Well, I'll read the book you gave me."

"Don't read it to be polite. Only read it if you like it. The world is filled with good books."

"The world is filled with exciting things to do, too. Let's go."

He drove the car he'd rented to a restaurant a few streets away. The place had soft lights, dark paneling, a piano player and linen-covered tablecloths with pink rosebuds in vases on each table.

Wyatt ordered steaks for them and was charming through dinner. At one point she asked him, "How was your business deal today?"

"Not what I'd hoped in some ways, but I did make the sale and I'm rid of an albatross."

"Why did you tell me to go out and spend money when you didn't know whether you would get the money you wanted from this deal?"

He smiled at her and reached across the table to take her hand. "Because the money I made today doesn't matter. Grace, I had more money than my dad from my businesses in California. Then I inherited all the Sawyer properties and businesses.''

She stared at him wide-eyed. ''That's wonderful, Wyatt. Megan will be well provided for, then.''

''There are a lot of women I would never tell one word about my finances, but you I can tell. First of all you have a healthy appreciation for money. At the same time, that doesn't make me have one iota more appeal to you, does it.''

''No. Your money really doesn't have anything to do with how much you appeal to me.'' She smiled. ''But you probably don't believe that, in spite of what you just said.''

''I do believe it. Your values aren't the same as those of a lot of people.''

''Might not be. But I do appreciate money. Except I hope you don't spoil Megan when she's older.''

''I hope by then I'll have a wife who'll keep me from it.''

''I thought you didn't ever want to marry.''

''Life changes. I'm changing. You and Megan are changing me.''

The piano player had been joined by three more musicians, and several couples began to dance. Wyatt stood and took her hand. ''Dance with me.''

Grace walked to the dance floor and into his arms. Wyatt held her lightly, his hand holding hers and his other hand in the small of her bare back. As they danced together, she gazed up with her wide, green eyes, and his pulse thrummed. He wanted to pull down her hair, kiss her, peel her out of that bit of a dress.

He knew she didn't want to be a live-in lover. He suspected that in spite of yielding to his kisses, she might stick with what she said. But he also thought he could seduce her. He wanted her as he had never wanted any other woman. But he wanted more than just a lover. He wanted her friendship. He wanted her with him at the end of the day. Today he'd liked having her with him on this jaunt.

Marriage. Something he'd always said he didn't want, but now he did. He always thought marriage would take away his freedom, but he didn't want to be free from Grace.

He promised himself that he wouldn't rush into proposing to her until he was sure of his feelings, but he grew more certain by the hour. He hadn't known her a long time, yet each day added to his desire to have her in his life. She constantly surprised him. She was a great companion. She was gorgeous, sexy, intelligent. And she was wonderful with Megan.

He circled the small dance floor with Grace, still gazing into her eyes, forgetting his surroundings and everything else except her. She was light in his arms, following his lead perfectly. He was too aware of the warm skin on the small of her back. He was on fire with wanting her.

He suspected if he did something she really didn't like, she would quit working for him. "You know how to dance, Grace. Who've you dated?"

"No one important. Who've you dated?" she shot back.

"No one important," he answered, and she smiled.

The music changed to a fast number and she was equally adept at that. She must have dated someone sometime, gone dancing with him a lot, a thought he didn't care to dwell on. The next slow number, he couldn't resist. "You're a great dancer. You've dated enough to get that mastered."

She smiled at him. "Jealous, Wyatt?"

Surprised, he stared at her and then laughed. "I guess so."

"Well, you don't need to be. I'm from a strong church family, remember? I've spent a thousand hours at Sunday-school dances and church-sponsored events that included dancing."

"Now that's good news. I don't remember feeling any kind of jealousy before."

"Phooey. I find that difficult to believe."

"It's true," he said, pulling her closer.

They danced until dusk, and he knew they should start home. Reluctantly he led her from the dance floor, and in minutes they were speeding to the airport and boarding his jet.

She was fascinated by their takeoff, looking at the twinkling lights of Houston below and exclaiming in delight.

"Could it be that you like flying?" he asked.

She turned to smile at him. "The weather is perfect. I figured you would know what you're doing, so it's okay. It's still risky, but not high risk. And you told me you have a will and a guardian appointed for Megan, so she's covered if something happens. This seems safer than your motorcycle. That I'll never like."

"Bet you ride on it with me."

"Bet I don't."

"I withdrew from the bull-riding competition in California."

She turned to stare at him. "Why?"

"Why do you think?"

"Because of me? Because I don't approve of it? I don't think so, Wyatt. Why did you?"

"I can give up some of my activities. I canceled the skydiving I had scheduled. That one I can give up easily. In the future, I thought I'd switch from bull riding to bronc riding. Broncs aren't as dangerous as bulls. I have one more—I can't get out of bull riding in the rodeo in San Antonio."

She stared at him, and he had to smile. "Speechless?"

"Yes, I am. You don't mind giving up those things?"

"Nope, or I wouldn't have done it. I care what you think."

"Oh, my!" she exclaimed.

"Don't look so totally undone. Isn't that what you wanted?"

"It's what I think is best for Megan because you're her daddy now, but I'm amazed you'd do it just like that."

"Megan doesn't give a rip if I ride bulls or jump out of airplanes. That wasn't why I did it," he said quietly.

"Wyatt, I'm stunned. You can't have done that for me. We're not that important to each other."

"Well, I did do it for you, and you're getting to be important in my life. I should have told you all this when I wasn't having to keep my attention on piloting this plane."

"You keep flying. Thank you, I guess."

They lapsed into silence, and then he changed the subject, asking her about her shopping.

It was eleven before they picked up a sleeping Megan and drove home, then put her to bed.

Wyatt tiptoed out of the nursery and switched off lights. He caught Grace's hand. "Come downstairs and have a drink with me."

"It's been a wonderful day and night, Wyatt. I had a marvelous time and thank you for the dress, but I should say good-night now."

He swung her up in his arms and carried her into her bedroom, setting her on her feet and wrapping his arms around her waist. "I get a good-night kiss," he said in a husky voice. He leaned down to kiss her and she wrapped her arms around his neck.

"You're so beautiful," he whispered. "Grace, I want you. You're going to be mine."

"This is all wrong," she whispered. "You should go right now."

"You don't like to kiss?" he asked, kissing her and tightening his arms around her. He wanted to devour her. He wanted to love her the whole night long and felt there was nothing wrong about anything involving her.

Grace trembled, knowing she should be strong and send him on his way, but she couldn't. She'd never known a man like Wyatt, and she knew she never would again. She wanted his loving, wanted him. She couldn't resist his kisses. She stopped arguing with herself, flinging aside worries momentarily and tightening her arms around his neck to kiss him back.

He was trembling, too, and she was startled by the knowledge, just as she had been surprised earlier to learn he was giving up some of his dangerous activities. *For her.* That was what was so stunning, though she hadn't fully accepted that he'd changed his life for her alone. Was it something temporary? Something he would regret later? Or go back to later? If he had quit permanently, she was awed, amazed and frightened that she had become that important to him.

In spite of great times together or compatibility or wild, passionate kisses that set them both on fire, he was not the man for her and she wasn't the woman for him. He wasn't the marrying kind, and even if he was, she didn't want to tie her life to a daredevil. He had changed some, but he wasn't ever going to change completely. He'd never stop riding his motorcycle or flying or riding wild animals or myriad other things that involved risk. And he would become bored with her quiet ways.

But right now, however fleeting, was so incredible! She stopped thinking, just lost herself in a dizzying spiral of sensation. She felt his hand on her back and before she knew it, her dress was puddled on the floor at her feet. She wore only panties and panty hose now, and Wyatt inhaled sharply, leaning back to cup and caress her breasts in his warm hands and gaze at her. "You're so lovely," he whispered.

As his thumbs circled her nipples, she trembled with desire. She fumbled with the buttons of his shirt, pushing it away and running her hands over his marvelous chest.

Then he was embracing her again, kissing her wildly. She wound her fingers into his hair, aware of his hands in her hair, pulling down her curls.

She struggled for reason, for sanity. She had to stop and he had to stop. She pushed against his chest. "Wyatt, wait."

He straightened. His breathing was raspy, and the desire in his eyes made her heart thud.

"Wyatt, we have to stop. I'm not ready to go further. I can't."

He leaned down to take a breast in his mouth, stroking her nipple with his tongue.

She gasped, moaning softly with pleasure, holding his strong shoulders. "Wyatt—"

He straightened again. "You're the most beautiful

woman I've ever known, Grace,'' he said solemnly. ''I want you more than I've ever wanted anyone.''

''Oh, Wyatt, don't. We don't belong together.''

''I don't know why you think that. But if you want me to go, I will.''

''I do want you to leave. I'm not ready for this.''

He clamped his lips together, turned and was gone.

Grace moved to the door, leaning her forehead against it and hurting. Tears stung her eyes. She wanted Wyatt. Every inch of her body ached for him. She would never again know a man like him. He had brought excitement, joy, exuberance into her life. He was the sexiest man she would ever know. Yet she couldn't be his lover, couldn't involve herself with him.

She knew she'd done the right thing. If she had good sense, she would quit this job, yet the thought of leaving Megan and Wyatt tore at her.

She heard the roar of the motorcycle and knew he was leaving on one of his midnight rides. She picked up her dress and moved stiffly around the room. Her body ached for him, for his hands and mouth and lovemaking.

She pulled on her nightie and sat in a chair by the window. An hour later she saw him return. He was bare-chested, speeding up the drive and whipping in a circle to stop and climb off.

''I love you, Wyatt Sawyer,'' she whispered, knowing she had indeed fallen in love with him. Hopelessly in love. They didn't have a future, but she couldn't change her heart.

Take him as a lover, an inner voice urged. Just once. She would never know lovemaking the way she would with Wyatt. She shook her head in the darkened room. If she gave herself to him, how would she ever get over him? She wasn't certain she was going to, anyway. If they made love, how could she work with him daily, knowing such intimacy?

"Wyatt, you've complicated my life," she whispered.

Outside, Wyatt strode across a field heading for the horses, then swung onto the bare back of his bay to ride to the gate. He slipped off and opened the gate, whistled the horse through and closed the gate, then jumped on again. He locked his hands in the mane and urged the horse forward, riding without seeing, his thoughts lost on Grace while he waited for his body to cool down.

He wanted her.

He thought about her full breasts, touching them tonight. His body burned with desire for her. But it went deeper than desire—was this really love?

What could he do Saturday night? Where could he take her that would be special? Could he get someone to keep Megan again? He needed to find a nanny so he could go out with his nanny.

He wouldn't sleep tonight. Images of Grace taunted him. Memories plagued him. Imagination set him on fire.

He rode for an hour, then went to the barn to feed, water and brush his horse, finally turning him out to pasture again.

Later, Wyatt sprawled in bed and opened his new book to read, munching some of the chocolates Grace had given him. It was almost dawn before he fell into a fitful sleep filled with dreams of Grace.

The next morning he picked up the mail from the day before and carried it to the kitchen to join Megan and Grace. It was Mrs. Perkins's day off and Grace had cooked a breakfast of eggs and toast. She sat feeding Megan. Wyatt's gaze slipped over both of them, and his brows arched. "Grace, I thought I told you to get some other clothes yesterday."

"I did. That black dress was new. As far as what I wear when I'm working, my clothes are just fine. I'm not spending your money to buy shorter skirts and tighter blouses."

He grinned at her and sat at the kitchen table, plopping the mail down in front of him. "Scared you'll get me all hot and bothered if you do?"

"No. It just seems a ridiculous waste of money when I have a closet of nice clothes."

Wyatt opened an envelope, staring at the contents before he started swearing.

Grace glanced at him. "I'm glad Megan can't understand you." One look at Wyatt's face, and she knew she shouldn't joke with him. "What's wrong, Wyatt?"

"Olivia's parents want my lawyer and me to meet with them. They want custody of Megan."

Nine

"**I** can't believe it! You told me that you called them and said they could come see her."

"I did and they said fine and that's the last I've heard until this." He waved the letter. "They've shown no interest in her. Hank told me that they seldom saw Megan."

"They can't get custody, can they?"

"I don't know. I'll have to talk to Prentice. I'll fight them as long and as hard as I can."

"What about Olivia, their daughter? Did she have a will?"

"Yes. She and Hank had identical wills and she named me as Megan's guardian, too. Olivia didn't want them as guardians."

"It would be a crime for them to take Megan from you."

He smiled at Grace. "I don't think they can. I'll go call my lawyer now."

"Do you have a good lawyer? You haven't lived here long."

"I think so. Prentice Bolton was Hank's attorney, and his firm is highly recommended by a lot of people I deal with. He's Gabe Brant's lawyer, too."

"Good."

As Wyatt left the room, she gazed after him and then hugged Megan, saying a swift prayer for Megan and Wyatt.

Wyatt made an appointment to see his lawyer that afternoon. He left for his office, and Grace and Megan were alone.

Grace waited that night to eat with Wyatt. She heard his car arrive and in minutes he came striding into the house, crossing the room to pick up Megan and hug her. She squealed with delight.

It wasn't until they were seated over baked chicken that Grace brought up the custody question. "What did your lawyer say today?"

"He said not to worry. Olivia and Hank had solid wills."

"Good! Do you still have to meet with the Volmers?"

"Sure. We have to go through the motions. If we can't work things out, they can take me to court, but hopefully, it'll be dropped before then. Now, what happened here today?"

"I took Megan to Stallion Pass with me and I got our pictures." She reached behind her to retrieve the envelope and then handed it to him.

Wyatt pulled out the pictures taken the day he'd come home from work and found Grace playing with Megan, making her laugh. As he ran through the stack of pictures,

Grace watched him. He was still in a white shirt and jeans. His hair was a tangle above his forehead and with summer, his skin was getting deeply tanned.

"Nice pictures," he said, smiling and handing them back to her. "Grace, will you go to dinner with me Saturday night? I have a sitter lined up for Megan."

Torn between wanting to accept and knowing she should refuse, Grace stared at him. "Wyatt—"

"Come on. Just dinner and dancing. Wear your pretty black dress, or go buy another one."

She laughed. "I don't need another dress! All right, Wyatt, but you know as well as I do that we shouldn't date. It'll only lead to trouble."

"If it's trouble, then it's the best kind of trouble," he said softly. "Seven o'clock, Saturday night. Okay?"

"Okay. Who's watching Megan?"

"Jorene Ryder. She's one of Ashley's cousins, and Gabe and Ashley have used her before. She said just to bring Megan to her house, because she has sisters who will help. Then we'll pick Megan up on the way home."

"Wyatt, it's crazy for us to date."

"It would be crazier for us not to. You'll see. You'll have a good time Saturday night."

"That's what's worrying me."

He grinned. "Try life on the wild side and see what my world is like." He strode out of the room whistling a cheerful tune, and she stared at his back in consternation. He could get her tied in knots while he was enjoying himself on a trail to seduction.

"Try life on the wild side and see what my world is like." His words rang in her ears. Maybe she should. At least a degree more than she usually did.

That afternoon she buckled Megan into the carrier in the back seat of the car and drove to San Antonio. Laurie

Kellogg had told her about dress shops there. Grace shopped for about an hour and then returned home, this time buying a red dress with her own money.

That night she awoke to Megan's cries. They had agreed she would get up weeknights with Megan and Wyatt would take the weekends, so she rolled out of bed. Since that first night, she had never again seen Wyatt in the nursery and so had long ago stopped throwing on a robe. Besides, her cotton nightgown covered her from chin to toes.

She picked up Megan and switched on a small light. She changed her diaper and then went to the kitchen to get a bottle, returning to Megan's room to sit and rock her.

Megan finished the bottle and Grace quietly rocked until the baby was asleep. She carried her to bed. "Good night, sweet baby. You're my little love. I love you, Megan," she said softly, and leaned over the crib to kiss the baby.

"Need help?"

Startled, she looked up. Wyatt stood in the doorway. He was bare-chested, dressed only in jeans that had the top button unfastened. As he came into the room, her pulse jumped and she clutched the neck of her nightgown.

"No, she's asleep now. I thought I was the one getting up on weeknights."

"I couldn't sleep." He stopped beside Grace and looked at the sleeping baby. "I never knew I could love someone the way I love her."

"You're a good daddy, Wyatt."

He raised his head and her heart thudded as his dark eyes met hers. Desire was obvious in the dark depths.

"She's asleep now. Come here," he said, taking

Grace's hand and walking backward toward his bedroom door.

"Wyatt—"

"Shh, Grace, just for a minute."

She slipped her wrist out of his grasp. "I'm going to bed, Wyatt," she said.

He caught her around the waist and pulled her to him. "Don't be in such a rush," he whispered. He leaned down to kiss her.

What good did it do to protest? Every time, she not only yielded to his kisses, she returned them.

"Ah, Grace," he said, holding her head with one hand while his other arm banded her waist and he kissed her deeply. He walked backward, a silent, slow dance to passion, and then they were in his bedroom. He closed the door behind them.

His hand went to her breast, stroking the taut peak through her nightgown. She felt his fingers at the buttons and then he slipped his hand beneath her gown to cup her breast and stroke her nipple with his thumb.

She moaned softly, pleasure rippling through her. Tonight, she thought, love him tonight. Take his loving and let it be a memory forever. Yet if she did, could she live under the same roof with him and ever again say no to him?

Questions were dim, like annoying bees buzzing nearby, and growing dimmer with each caress and kiss.

He framed her face with his hands and looked at her intently. "I love you, Grace."

Her heart thudded violently and she stared at him. Then she remembered it was Wyatt, the man with a past filled with women. Words of love probably rolled off his tongue as easily as breathing.

Words that even if they'd been true, would never

change one iota of the circumstances between them. An impossible situation. Yet tonight, just tonight, she wanted to know him fully.

"You can't love me," she whispered.

"Yes, I can and I do," he said. "I love you," he repeated, and pulled her close and kissed away any reply. His kisses escalated. Hot, demanding, never-to-be-forgotten kisses that burned away every thought in her head. She clung to him, kissing him in return while her body ached for his loving.

"I want to take all night to pleasure you, Grace." He caught her gown and with a twist, it was over her head and tossed aside.

His broad chest expanded as he inhaled. His gaze was a caress, trailing over her scalding body. His hands rested on her waist as he leaned down to take her nipple in his mouth, to stroke the bud with his tongue.

She clung to him, running her hands through his hair and across his strong shoulders. His body was a wonder to her, something to discover and relish. He peeled away his jeans and stepped out of them, then pushed away his briefs.

Wyatt picked her up to carry her to his bed, coming down over her to trail kisses across her flat stomach to her breasts.

He moved between her legs and his hands drifted lightly over her, feathery touches that left trails of fire. And then he kissed her leg, behind her knee, letting his tongue slide up her inner thigh, his hot breath on her while he watched her.

She was far beyond the point of going back. Tonight he would make love to her as much and as long as he wanted to. And then his hand caressed her intimately, rubbing and stroking, taking her to a peak as she clung to him and cried out, wanting him beyond her wildest dreams.

She pushed him down and moved over him, showering kisses over his muscled chest, his throat, his ear and then down across his flat belly, down, stroking his thighs, breathing so lightly over his thick shaft, touching him with slow caresses that made him shake and gasp.

He came off the bed to turn them so he was above her, kissing her again, his hands everywhere, giving her pleasure every way he could.

He ran his hands through her hair. "You're beautiful, Grace. I can't ever look at you enough. Sexy, gorgeous."

He turned her onto her stomach and began to caress and kiss her back, moving down, his hands stroking her bottom, moving over her thighs and the backs of her knees.

With a cry she twisted and turned over to sit up, taking his shaft in her hand. She kissed him, stroked him, tried to pleasure him until he groaned and pulled her into his embrace. He cradled her in his arms, leaning over her and kissing her with unbridled passion, kisses to make her faint, kisses to make her want him more than anything else in life.

He pushed her down, moving between her legs again. As Grace looked at him, her breath caught. He was aroused, ready, a male in his prime filled with sexual energy. Her heart thudded in anticipation.

Wyatt took a deep breath, looking at Grace. She was ready, eager for him. He felt he would burst with his love and need for her. He wanted her to be his woman, wanted to love her senseless, wanted to share everything with her. Never had he felt like this.

"Wyatt, I want you!" she exclaimed, and sat up to pull him to her and kiss him.

Wyatt shifted, and moved away to retrieve a packet
and when he returned, his gaze held hers steadily. His
mouth covering hers as he kissed her hard, shoving her
back down on the bed and lowering himself over her.

She watched him, running her hands along his strong
thighs. Then she wrapped her arms around him when he
lowered himself between her legs. His shaft touched her,
teasing, touching.

"Wyatt!" she cried. "Please!"

"I want you to want me like you've never wanted
anything or anyone before."

"I do! Come here."

He kissed her, stopping her words. He entered her
slowly and she gasped, but her cry was muffled, taken
with his kisses.

Grace thought she would faint with need, wanting all
of him, needing to move, to satisfy this urgency he had
built inside her.

Hot and hard, he filled her slowly. She locked her legs
around him, rocking with him, wanting him, needing release. Tension built as he moved in.

"Wyatt!" she cried before his mouth again muffled
her cries.

Wyatt felt the tightness, knew she was a virgin. He
tore his mouth from hers. "I don't want to hurt you."

"Wyatt, love me," she whispered, her hands on his
firm buttocks, her legs pulling him closer.

Sweat rolled off him as he tried to go slowly, to build
her up to a frenzy, but then his control slipped away and
he thrust inside her, going deep, covering her mouth with
his to take her cry.

They moved together and she was abandoned in his
arms, thrashing and twisting, driving him beyond conscious thought. All control had vanished, hers and his.

And she was in as big a frenzy as he was. When release burst in him, Wyatt shuddered, pumping and relishing her passionate responses.

He never knew how long before they slowed. Both of them quieted, gasping for breath, their hearts pounding together. He showered kisses on her, knowing that for the first time in his life, he was truly in love.

Grace clung to Wyatt, feeling his hard length stretched against her. They were one, united, and for this moment, he loved her with all his body. And maybe, for now, with all his heart.

He was the first man in her life and, she suspected, the only one forever. She was as certain of her love for him as she was of its hopelessness.

Running her hands over his strong back, she pushed away her thoughts. Time for reality tomorrow. Tonight she was in Wyatt's arms and she wanted his loving, his kisses. She wanted to touch and feel his body, to revel in his lovemaking.

Wyatt kissed her throat, her temple. Then he rolled over, holding her close and keeping her in his arms, his legs wrapped around her. He smiled at her. "You're perfect."

"Oh, Wyatt, I didn't know it could be like this!" she exclaimed, tightening her arms around him.

He kissed her again and then raised his head. "It will get a lot better than this. You'll see. What we have, Grace, is special. So incredibly special."

She placed her fingers on his lips. "Stop talking, Wyatt. Take the moment and keep tomorrow shut away for now."

"Suits me fine," he whispered, still showering her with light kisses, his hands trailing over her. "I want to memorize every inch of you, kiss every inch of you, love every inch of you. You're gorgeous, Grace.''

"You're crazy or blind. That wasn't your first impression of me.''

"I guess not, since you did everything you could to hide your beauty.'' He leaned away to smile at her, stroking damp tendrils of hair from her face. "This is paradise.''

"Yes, it is.''

"You're my woman now, Grace. Mine.''

She stroked his face, feeling the rough stubble on his jaw. His hair fell in a tangle over his forehead, black locks curling damply. There was a fine sheen of sweat on his shoulders and chest and she ran her hands lightly over him. "It goes both ways, Wyatt. I can't get enough of touching you. This magic night is a special treasure.''

"You're the special treasure,'' he whispered. "It's never, ever been like this. Not once, not ever.''

While her heart skipped beats, she tightened her arms around him, placing her head against his chest and listening to the steady rhythm of his heart.

He stroked her back, running his hands from her shoulder to her bottom and then up again, while his other arm banded her waist. "I don't want you out of my arms tonight,'' he whispered. "I want to know that you're here, letting me love you. I've dreamed of this, Grace, since that first night.''

"You can't have!''

"Oh, yes, I did.''

"Well, that was nothing but lust.''

"Might have been, but it's more than lust now. Did you know that I haven't had a peaceful night's sleep since I inherited Megan—first because of her and then because of you.''

"I don't believe you," Grace said, raising her head.

He held up his hand, palm toward her. "I swear it's the truth."

"I don't know why. I did everything I could to keep you from noticing me. At least now you can sleep peacefully."

"Why do I doubt that?" He shifted slightly. "I'm re-energized. Let's get in the tub."

"You're crazy, Wyatt."

"You'll see. We'll have a great time." He stood and scooped her up in his arms and carried her into the bathroom. In minutes he was in the tub seated behind her with his arms and legs wrapped around her while he soaped her all over. "How's this? Pretty good, huh?"

"Mmm, better than books," she murmured, closing her eyes while he rubbed her back lightly with a warm, wet cloth.

"Better than chocolate, too," he said huskily. "I love your hair," he added. He played with her curls while he soaped her back with his free hand.

As he rinsed her off, she closed her eyes, relishing the relaxing rub, the warm water, and Wyatt wrapped around her. When he reached around with his hand to stroke a nipple, she inhaled swiftly. "Wyatt!"

"You feel so good," he whispered, cupping her breasts in his wet hands and caressing them. Gasping, she closed her eyes, leaning back and twisting around to kiss him.

In minutes she turned, and he moved her over him, settling her on his manhood, holding her tightly while they moved together.

Her eyes closed, Grace returned his kisses and clung to him until she cried out her release. Then she felt his shuddering release. She sprawled against him and he held her tightly, stroking her hair and murmuring soft endearments.

Thirty minutes later they were back in bed, wrapped in each other's arms. Through the night Wyatt loved her, and she was amazed at his energy and stamina.

Near dawn she lay in his arms. The night had been bliss and she didn't want it to end, but she knew it must.

She turned to look at him. He lay on his side with one arm beneath her and the other arm wrapped around her waist. His dark lashes were feathery shadows above his prominent cheekbones. She smoothed locks of his black hair away from his forehead. She loved him and she would love him the rest of her life. The knowledge hurt because their lifestyles and their futures were poles apart.

He had told her he loved her, but she didn't take him seriously. He had been in the throes of passion, and she suspected he had told a fair number of women the same thing. She didn't want to think about that. Right now she just wanted to cherish Wyatt and the night and moments that had already become memories.

She kissed his head lightly, trying to keep from waking him, yet unable to stop touching him. She shifted and found herself looking into his dark-brown eyes.

"I didn't mean to wake you," she whispered.

"I'm glad you did. I have something I bought for you when I was in town this week. Don't go away. Promise."

"I promise," she replied with amusement, wondering if he thought she might get up and run to her room the moment he let go of her.

She watched him walk across the room casually as if unaware of his nudity. His body was male perfection. Tanned, rippling muscles, lean and hard. Her mouth went dry and her pulse began to race as she looked at him, and she wanted him again, wanted to hold him, wanted to feel his body against hers, wanted his loving.

He fished something from a drawer and returned. She saw that he was aroused again, a perpetual state through the night. She held out her arms, wanting him, his gift forgotten.

He lowered himself to the bed and pulled her close. "I love you."

"I love you," she replied solemnly in return, stroking his cheek.

"Grace, will you marry me?" he asked, and held out a ring.

Ten

Stunned, she stared at the ring that sparkled in the glow of the one small lamp. She sat up, staring at Wyatt in amazement.

"Wyatt, this is so sudden."

"It might be sudden to you, but I've been thinking about it for some time. It never takes me long to make up my mind about what I want. Especially something I want badly."

Everything in her cried out to throw her arms around him and say yes. But wisdom said no. A lump formed in her throat, and tears stung her eyes.

"What happened to all that freedom you said you cherished?" she asked.

"I wanted freedom from people I didn't love. It's different when you love someone. My freedom is with you in my life. I don't want to be away from you. I want you part of my life always."

"Oh, Wyatt! We're so incredibly different! I love you and you're wonderful and maybe I'll always love you."

He frowned. "I'm not getting the reaction I'd hoped for here. What's wrong? You told me you loved me. I love you. It's pretty simple to me."

She shook her head. "I can't accept."

"Why not, Grace?" he asked, his heart plunging. An ache started and he wondered if it would ever end.

"I've told you before—our lifestyles. You can't change completely for me and I can't change completely for you."

"Can't we go on like we are now? We've been doing just fine together."

"Wyatt, the more I love you, the more I worry about you. When you go out the door, I worry about you. I don't want to go through life like that. And I don't want you to change for me. You wouldn't be happy."

"Ah, hell, Grace. I've given up skydiving and bull riding. I don't take chances like I used to. And when you've flown with me, you liked it. Tell me you didn't."

"It was fine, Wyatt, but the weather was good. We didn't take Megan with us. If I marry you, I'll be a mother to her and I won't be able to stand watching you teach her to fly and ride and do all those things."

"It's life. It's just living."

"What you do is more than just living. It's life on the wild side. You drive too fast. You ride that motorcycle without a helmet. I just know that there'd be endless arguments and worry and neither of us would be happy."

"I think I could be very happy," he said solemnly. Her words hurt him, and he thought she was being foolish and ridiculous. She had already changed a lot since she'd moved to the ranch. And he had changed.

"I can't say yes. I just can't."

"We're both changing," he argued. Her tumble of curls framed her face and cascaded over her silky shoulders. She had the sheet tucked beneath her arms, and it clung to her curves. One long leg was out from under the sheet. She looked lovely to him and he ached with wanting her.

"But we're not changing enough," she answered sadly.

He wiped away her tears. "I've never really been in love before. Not like this. This is going to hurt, Grace. It's going to hurt badly."

"It does hurt."

"Well, it's needless. I'll try to keep from worrying you. Maybe after you've lived out here awhile, you'll get used to some of the things I do. But I can't sit in the house on summer evenings with my nose in a book."

They stared at each other and then he pulled her into his arms to kiss her as if he'd been deprived of kisses for a year, instead of only minutes. He bent over her, his demanding kiss silencing their argument, making her heart pound as she wrapped her arms around him and responded.

Wyatt wanted to devour her. To drive all the doubts away and make her see that they belonged together. He needed Grace with every fiber of his being. He was incomplete without her. And yet he couldn't alter his entire life. And he couldn't expect her to alter hers. He wondered now if he was really kissing her goodbye.

In spite of the tears that streamed down her cheeks, Grace clung to him until finally she pushed against him and he released her. "I can't, Wyatt. I just know I can't. But I do love you."

She slipped out of bed, grabbing her nightgown and rushing back through the nursery door. She crossed the room to the crib, looking at Megan and knowing she was saying no to Megan, as well as to Wyatt. She would lose them both.

Fresh tears streamed down her cheeks. "Marry him. Take a chance on Wyatt and life. You'll have Megan," she whispered to herself, but she thought about the future and knew she would be in knots every time Wyatt went on his bike or flew or rode a bronc. And she couldn't bear to think of him teaching Megan that lifestyle.

She went to her room and sat in the dark, wanting to hold Wyatt and be in his arms, wanting to hold Megan. She loved them both, but how could she let go of feelings and worries she'd had for a lifetime?

If she married Wyatt, she was afraid that in time, they would be unhappy with each other. He didn't like books or the things she did. He wouldn't want to do the things she liked. She would hate some of the things he liked to do. She wouldn't want him taking Megan with him.

Grace rubbed her temples. Her head had started to throb. She loved Wyatt with all her heart, but that didn't change daily living and what they each liked to do.

Could she adapt to his ways? Could she let go of worries and fears and her conservative lifestyle? Could she give up some of the things she loved so deeply? She didn't think she could change enough.

And she was certain Wyatt couldn't.

So how could she stay here if she didn't?

She looked at the closed door to Megan's room. She adored that child.

The thought of Wyatt wanting to take Megan on his bike with him sent chills through her. She would never adjust to that. She knew she had to find another job and move away from Wyatt, Megan and the ranch.

The realization hurt. Her head throbbed more than ever

and she couldn't stop crying. She wanted Wyatt and Megan and the glittering, wonderful life he offered, but it would never work.

She would have to leave. Unless she accepted his proposal, there was no way she could stay. And the sooner she left, the easier it would be on all of them.

Grace hurt so much she could barely breathe. How could love hurt like this? Wyatt was wonderful and marvelous and terrifying all at the same time. He seemed to have no fear of anything.

She stared into the gray early dawn, still crying and hurting and wanting to run back into his arms. She moved to the bed and cried herself to sleep.

A couple of hours later she heard Megan. She climbed out of bed and went to get her. Holding her close, she murmured, "I love you, Megan. You'll never know how much. I want to marry your daddy and live with both of you. But I don't think we could last, and when I marry, I want it to be forever."

She put Megan on a blanket on the floor while she swiftly dressed, and then she took her downstairs. Grace's pulse jumped at the prospect of seeing Wyatt, but it seemed he was already gone. A note was propped on the table.

"See you at dinner," was written in his bold scrawl.

She picked up the note and put it in her pocket, wanting him, wanting to kiss him, wanting him to hold her. Was she making the most foolish mistake of her life?

Yet every time she thought about Megan growing up and Wyatt teaching her to do the daredevil things he did, Grace knew she could never learn to tolerate it or avoid continually worrying and constantly arguing with Wyatt.

She would help Wyatt hire another nanny, so he wouldn't have to go through all those interviews again.

It hurt to think about getting another nanny, but Grace knew that was the only thing to do. She would tell him when he got home tonight.

"I love you, Megan," she said through her tears, picking up the baby to hug her.

The day seemed a thousand hours long to Grace, but she began to make plans to move.

Wyatt called once while she was in the yard with Megan. He left a terse message that he would be late, and she wondered if he was staying away on purpose. She knew she had hurt him and she was sorry. She suspected he would rebound far better than she would.

That night he wasn't home until late, and Megan had already gone to bed. When he came in, Grace was reading in the family room. Watching her solemnly, he dropped his jacket on a chair and crossed to her.

Her pulse jumped as he approached. He leaned down, taking her hands and pulling her to her feet. As she stood, he put his arms around her. "I missed you and I hope you've thought about my proposal and our future."

She wound her arms around his neck and kissed him hungrily. He tightened his arms around her, kissing her hard, taking her breath and setting her aflame. She stopped thinking. For this moment she was back in Wyatt's arms, kissing him, holding him, and he was kissing her. A scalding urgency made her fingers shake as she peeled away his shirt.

Reason, fears, doubts, vanished. Desire and love were everything. Driven with need, she kissed him.

He pulled her T-shirt over her head and tossed it aside, unclasping her lacy bra to drop it, then cup her breasts. He bent to take a nipple into his mouth.

She shook with need, unbuckling his belt and then unfastening his slacks. They fell in a heap around his ankles. Releasing her, he sat on the sofa and peeled off his boots and then the rest of his clothes. He caught her wrist to pull her to him.

She sat on his lap, feeling his thick shaft pressing against her bare hip. Retrieving a packet for protection, he shifted her to the sofa and moved between her legs.

He was virile, so incredibly sexy, ready for her. As he entered her slowly, she arched to meet him.

"Wyatt, love me!" she gasped, wanting this moment because she didn't think there would be many more times like this. And she wanted to give herself to Wyatt, give him memories to last a lifetime. She tightened her legs around him, clinging to his strong back, moving with him.

If only...

She knew she couldn't follow the reasoning of other possibilities. They couldn't marry. It was that simple. She tasted salty tears, certain that this time she was telling him goodbye.

He lowered himself, entering her, and desire scalded her as she held him. He kissed her passionately, and then they were caught in an urgency that built until she thought she would explode with her need for him.

"I love you, Grace!" he cried out.

"Wyatt, oh, my love," she said, clinging to him and moving wildly with him.

Release came in a burst of ecstasy, then she felt his shuddering release.

As they slowed, their breathing gradually became natural. He crushed her to him, showering kisses on her, murmuring endearments. "Marry me, darlin'. It'll be so good between us, Grace. I love you."

"I love you, too, Wyatt," she whispered, kissing him.

In minutes he shifted and moved. "When I get the

strength, I'll carry you upstairs and we can take a long, leisurely bath together.''

"I can walk upstairs by myself," she said, smiling at him, too aware that for the moment, they were skirting the subject of their future.

"Go run the water. I'll get a cold beer for myself and a glass of wine for you and be right there."

She didn't want to argue now, so she watched him grab his clothes and leave the room. She picked up her things and hurried upstairs, checking on Megan and then going to Wyatt's bathroom and running water.

They bathed, ate a late dinner, made love again and then long into the night as she lay in his arms, she asked him about his day.

"You don't want to know. What happened here?"

Grace sat up and pulled the sheet beneath her arms. "I've thought about the future. Wyatt, I always come back to the same thing."

He looked as if she'd struck him a hard blow. He grimaced and reached out to stroke her arm. "Dammit, Grace, I love you. Really love you. But I can't give up my flying and rodeos and my bike. I can't change, especially when, to me, it seems ridiculous. Live a little, Grace. Are you going to tell Megan and me goodbye because you're scared of life?"

His question hurt, but she nodded. "I'm scared of it the way you live it. I can't bear to go through life watching you do risky things."

While they stared at each other, a muscle worked in his jaw. "So where do we go from here? Live like this?"

"No, of course not. All day I've thought about it." She took a deep breath, knowing that with her next words, she would be telling him goodbye. "I'll help you hire a new nanny and then I'll leave."

She saw the pain in his expression. "Just like that, you're gone?"

"I don't see anything else we can do," she replied.

"Whatever happens, we need a new nanny, but if you move out, Grace, it's over."

"It was over before it started, Wyatt. I'm sorry. And we can't go out Saturday night." She slipped out of bed and reached for her robe, wrapping it around her and leaving without looking back. Tears streamed down her cheeks and she knew that this time they had truly said goodbye. Now they would just go through the motions and do the things necessary for her to move away.

She didn't know she could possibly hurt so badly. Half an hour later she heard the roar of the motorcycle.

Wyatt raced away into the night, tearing down the county road, letting the wind whip against him. After an hour he returned to the ranch. He needed to move, do something physical. He drove to the pasture where he kept the white stallion that he had named Legend. Taking out a bridle and saddle, he stood quietly, talking to the horse, which was a hundred yards away. Wyatt had worked with the stallion enough now that the horse was becoming accustomed to him.

Moonlight bathed the powerful animal as the two stared at each other. Wyatt turned and walked away, standing quietly, waiting, finally hearing the horse moving behind him. It was another half hour before he reached out to touch the horse.

He had ridden the stallion three times now without getting bucked off and knew he better focus on the horse because he was still dealing with a dangerous animal.

Two hours later, he drove back to the house and the moment he left the stallion, his thoughts jumped to Grace. In his life he had left some broken hearts behind, but they mended, and he suspected no one had ever been deeply in love with him.

He kept telling himself he would get over Grace, but he didn't believe it. It was the same as telling himself that in the future, he wouldn't need air to breathe. He loved her desperately. At the same time, he knew if he promised her he would change completely and do what she wanted, he would never be able to keep the promise.

Tears stung his eyes and he wiped at them angrily. How could it hurt this much to love someone? The day had been pure hell. His lawyer was trying to avoid having to go to court over custody of Megan, but Olivia's parents were being hateful. They wanted Megan, and in his lawyer's opinion, they wanted her trust fund and inheritance. Since Hank had always said they never had any interest in Megan, Wyatt wondered if Prentice was right.

Wyatt realized he was losing Grace and he was going to have to fight to keep from losing Megan.

As he sat on the porch, he tried to think what he needed to do next. Monday morning he had another appointment with Prentice Bolton. Tomorrow was the Fourth of July. He had intended to take Grace and Megan to a picnic at the country club in San Antonio and then watch fireworks afterward, but that was out of the question now. There was a little rodeo in Stallion Pass. He would go to that, get away from the ranch and Grace. He would run an ad for a nanny. Grace had said she would help him hire someone. The sooner he did, the better it would be, because it was going to tear them both up to live under the same roof.

He swore steadily, wondering if the hurt would ever end. He knew Grace well enough now to know that she would stick to what she said.

He knew he'd better put the hurt behind him, because

he had another big battle looming that might be the fight of his life. He couldn't change Grace, but he could fight for Megan.

In the next few days Grace saw little of Wyatt. She knew he was busy selling some of the businesses Hank had owned. He flew to California and was gone a week. During the time he was away, the ad for a nanny ran and Grace did the early interviews.

By the time Wyatt returned, she had five likely candidates for him to interview. And then the second day he was back, she interviewed a woman she thought was exactly what Wyatt wanted.

Sonya Madison was an older woman whose grandchildren were all in college, and she loved little children. She'd been a nanny for the past ten years and had excellent references. She had kindly blue eyes, wore bifocals and had white hair.

After an interview with Wyatt, Sonya was hired and agreed to begin work the following Monday. July was more than half over.

As soon as Sonya moved into the house, Grace could devote herself full-time to finding an apartment and a job in San Antonio. Grace rarely saw Wyatt these days. He kept late hours and left early. When they were together, the air was filled with tension. She loved him and wanted to be in his arms. All of this was dreadful, yet she continued with her plans.

Grace found an apartment in San Antonio and then a job in an accounting office. She packed and got ready for her move.

On Thursday she worked all day, cleaning and getting her apartment ready. When she returned to the ranch, she climbed the stairs. She wore cutoffs and sneakers and had her hair in a thick braid. Tendrils escaped and curled around her face.

She went to see Megan, tiptoeing into the room in case the baby was asleep.

Dressed in a white shirt and a navy suit, his tie loosened, Wyatt stood beside the crib holding Megan in his arms. When Grace entered, he looked up. She was startled to see that his eyes were filled with tears.

His lips thinned and a muscle worked in his jaw as he turned away. "I just came in to see her," he said gruffly.

"Wyatt, what's wrong?" Grace asked.

When he turned to face her, he had control of his emotions.

"Things just aren't going well. You want to see Megan?"

"Yes, but I can come back later."

"You can see her now." Crossing the room, he handed the baby to Grace. "Sonya has gone early for the weekend. I told her I could watch Megan."

"I can watch her for a while if you have something you want to do."

He nodded and left the room. Grace stared after him, thinking about his answer. What was bothering him?

She set Megan down with her toys, then sat on the floor to play with her. In another half hour she heard Wyatt leave in his pickup. Later Grace fed Megan and put her to bed. Too aware of the empty house, Grace showered and changed into fresh cutoffs, T-shirt and sneakers. She went downstairs to find Wyatt on the porch in the dark. He had a bottle of beer and sat with his feet propped on the porch rail.

"Can I join you?" she asked.

He stood and waved his hand. "Sure. Come out. Want something to drink?"

"I have iced tea." She sat in a chair near his and he sat back down, propping his booted feet on the rail again.

"Wyatt, what's wrong?"

"Doesn't concern you now, Grace," he said, and she realized he was beginning to shut her out of his life.

"I didn't mean to pry," she said, suddenly feeling he didn't want her sitting with him. She stood and started inside. "'Night, Wyatt."

"Sit down. I have to go to court next month. The custody battle is going full force. The Volmers want Megan, and they have the money and the law firm to pursue this. They say I'm an unfit father, and they're dredging up a lot of old stuff."

Appalled, Grace stared at him. "That's terrible! How can they say you're an unfit father? You're a wonderful father."

"You might have a biased view," he said dryly.

"Can't I testify about your fitness as a father?"

He turned his head to look at her. "I don't think so, but thanks."

"Why not?" she asked, hurting for him. "You don't want me to try to help you? Wyatt, don't let your anger at me get in the way of letting me help you."

"Grace, you're part of the problem. They've accused us of living together out here, parties—remember my party? I don't think you can say one thing that will help. Remember, they saw us together at the restaurant in San Antonio. But thanks. I'll tell Prentice you offered to testify."

"That's terrible! And so wrong. Surely they don't stand a chance."

"They're blood relatives, too. They've been married a long time. I'm single, considered wild and unpredictable, not daddy material. I'll fight it legally as long as I can, but Prentice said we may not be able to stop them. A lot depends on the judge we get. They have a big legal outfit from Austin. Prentice knows their lawyers.''

"I'm sorry," Grace said, still aghast.

Megan began to cry, her wails coming clearly over the intercom. "I'll get her," Wyatt said, rising to his feet. "'Night, Grace."

When he left, Grace thought she'd never felt so alone. She hurt for Wyatt and for herself. His losing Megan was too terrible to contemplate. He was an adoring, wonderful father.

She sat staring into the dark for hours, but Wyatt never returned, and finally she went to her room. She lay in bed in the dark, mulling over his situation, mulling over the possibility he might lose Megan.

All her life family had been the most important thing. Nothing else mattered. Now Wyatt and Megan had become her family—Wyatt had asked her to become family forever.

She couldn't walk out on them. Could she accept Wyatt as he was? If she stayed, she would have to. With some deep soul-searching, she knew she was willing to try. She understood fully that if she married Wyatt, she was going to have to accept him as he was, with all his wild ways. Deciding that she would, she wondered if she was too late. And after making her decision, her heart leaped with eagerness. She wanted to run to Wyatt right then.

Instead, she forced herself to think it over more, wanting to be certain. Eventually she fell asleep.

The next morning, after she'd showered and dressed, she went downstairs to search for Wyatt, but he had already left and she learned he had taken Megan to Ashley

Ryder's for the day. Mrs. Perkins was there to cook and clean, so Grace was free to go.

She hurried to her room to change, dressing in a short navy skirt and sleeveless navy blouse and high-heeled pumps. She looped and pinned her hair on her head, told Megan goodbye and left word with Sonya and Mrs. Perkins where they could find her.

She drove to Wyatt's San Antonio office, stopping in the lobby to call him. It took a few minutes until he answered because his secretary had long ago been told to put Grace straight through to him.

"Can I come see you now?"

"I have an appointment in fifteen minutes. If you're at the ranch, we'll have to make it this afternoon."

"I'm in the lobby of your building."

There was a momentary pause. "Come on up."

She rode to the top floor where Sawyer Enterprises, Incorporated, was located. She entered a spacious reception room with lush potted plants, thick rugs on polished hardwood floors and leather furniture. In seconds, she was told to go ahead into his office.

She opened the door to a corner office with floor-to-ceiling windows that looked out over the city. Wyatt stood behind a polished wood desk, and his gaze swept over her swiftly as she entered and closed the door behind her.

"What brings you here, Grace?"

She walked across the room. Every nerve she had was raw. She wanted to run and throw herself into his arms, but he had thrown up a wall between them.

His brows arched as she kept walking around his desk to him. She stopped only inches away, and her heart was thudding.

"Wyatt, you may have lost interest now, but if you haven't...I want to marry you."

Stunned, Wyatt stared at her. His heart pounded and he wasn't sure he'd heard her correctly. He had been trying to shut her out of his life, out of his mind and heart, yet he hadn't been able to even slightly. Now she stood gazing at him, her green eyes pulling at him, telling him she would marry him. But she was too solemn, her voice too full of regrets.

"What brings this on, Grace?" he asked, trying to stop thinking about the possibilities, feeling there was a catch somewhere. "Yesterday you wouldn't even consider marrying me."

Eleven

"**I**'m sorry. I know I hurt you," she said quietly. Her eyes filled with tears, which she wiped away swiftly before they fell. "I don't blame you and I know you've been trying to forget me."

"I believe you're the one trying to distance yourself from Megan and me as fast as you can."

"Wyatt, I thought about it all last night. Near morning I fell asleep, but I meant to catch you before you left for work today. Family has always been the most important thing in my life. We've never owned a home, never lived one place long, so I never had long friendships. Family was it. Now you and Megan are my family."

"I may lose her soon, Grace." His eyes narrowed. "You're doing this to help me keep from losing Megan, aren't you?"

"That was why I stopped to think about us and the future and the possibilities, but that isn't why I'm here.

If you could tell me right now that the custody suit was dropped, I'd still be here.''

''Why do I find that hard to believe?'' he said sharply, certain she was doing this to help him keep Megan. He was angry and hurt. He could fight his own battles, and he didn't want sympathy. ''All my life I've had to fight for what I wanted,'' he snapped. ''This isn't any different now, but I don't want your sympathy. Thank you, but no thanks. I've got an appointment.''

He turned away, putting papers in his briefcase, hurting and angry and aware she hadn't moved. Dammit. Why did she have to look so beautiful? He struggled, fighting every urge inside him to throw aside hurt feelings and worries and accept her offer.

When he turned around, she was gone. He felt as if his insides were crumbling into a million pieces. He thought he'd hurt as much as it was possible to hurt, but he'd been wrong.

That night when he got home, Grace had moved out. She had left a phone number and address, which Wyatt tossed into the trash.

With steely determination Grace drove to the Sawyer ranch on Saturday. She knew where to go and knew Wyatt was away for the afternoon because she had talked to his foreman, Jett Colby.

She reached the pasture that adjoined the road to the ranch house. This was where Legend was kept, and Grace stopped her car at the gate. At the sound of the engine, the stallion came trotting into view, his ears cocked forward.

''Watching for Wyatt, aren't you? We've both fallen under his spell,'' she said quietly as she opened the gate, drove inside and then got out to close the gate.

Wyatt had let her watch once when he had been working with the horse at the corral and she remembered every moment of that evening. She parked and got out, going around to open the trunk of her car and get out the saddle she had borrowed.

She looked at the horse. He stood watching her, his ears still cocked forward. She talked softly, getting out treats she had ready for him. She had spent the past two days at a San Antonio stable, learning about horses, how to saddle one, how to ride. She had decided to live life a little more fully and to stop being afraid of so many things. This seemed as good a place to start as any.

She waited patiently, knowing the horse was moving closer until he was finally only yards away. While she talked quietly to the horse, she turned to hold out her hand with apple slices. He moved closer and in minutes took the treat. She fished more out of a bag, held them out and then patted the horse.

Taking lots of time, she finally got a saddle on Legend and after a few more minutes, placed her foot in a stirrup and mounted him.

He shook his head and she realized she was trembling. "You can do this," she said to herself, patting his neck. She flicked the reins slightly and he began a sedate walk. She inhaled, wanting to get down, thrilled to be riding him, realizing maybe she should let go of so many worries and fears. If she could ride this horse, how much more likely for Wyatt to ride him without qualms. Of course, she knew Wyatt didn't care whether the horse was wild and hostile or docile.

She inhaled another deep breath, aware of the blue sky, the sun beating down on her above her floppy straw hat. She had worn a T-shirt, jeans and new boots. And she had plans to wear those boots again in a few more hours.

She ached with a terrible longing for Wyatt and then pulled her mind sharply back to the horse, knowing she needed to stay alert.

A pickup came along the road and too late, she realized she should have ridden away from the road and not toward it, but she knew from Wyatt's secretary that he had an afternoon appointment with his lawyer.

The pickup passed her, then turned and whipped off the road, bouncing over the ground toward the pasture gate.

She turned the horse to ride toward the gate, knowing that whoever it was, the driver was coming to see her.

The pickup stopped and Jett Colby climbed out, coming into the pasture. He stopped and stood at the gate.

"Grace, can you get down off that horse, please?"

She reined in and dismounted, leading the stallion with her until she was closer to Jett. "I just wanted to see if I could ride him."

"Grace, just drop the reins and get in your car and let me take it from here. I'll open the gate for you."

She smiled at Wyatt's foreman. "I can unsaddle him and I have some treats for him."

"You let me unsaddle him and forget the treats. Just get in your car. That horse is dangerous."

"You mean dangerous for an amateur. I've been out here a long time now," she said, glancing at her watch.

"Well, cut it short, please."

She heard the worry in his voice. With a glance at the horse, she turned and went to her car. She drove out and Jett opened the gate, closing it behind her. She cut the engine, stepped out and waited, watching Jett unsaddle Legend.

He carried the saddle and she opened the gate. He came through and put the saddle in the trunk of her car.

Suddenly the horse reared, pawing the air, whinnying loudly. He came down, pawing the earth, then turned and galloped across the pasture.

Jett turned to face her. "Grace, please don't ever ride him again—especially out here alone. He threw Wyatt last night and he's as unpredictable as spring weather. That's not a horse for you to be around at all. He may never be completely gentled."

"I just wanted to see if I could," she said. "I won't be out here again. Thanks for helping me."

"Sure," the older man said, his blue eyes studying her. "Wyatt is mighty unhappy. And he worries about losing Megan."

"That shouldn't ever happen."

"Nope, it shouldn't. Wyatt's a good daddy."

"Well, again, thanks. It was good to see you." She climbed into her car and started the engine, driving away and glancing in the rearview mirror to see Jett watching her.

Hot tears ran down her cheeks and she wiped them away angrily. "Wyatt, I love you," she whispered.

That night Wyatt slid onto the back of a bull at the rodeo in San Antonio. He wrapped the rope around his hand, but he didn't tie himself on. He had done that once and suffered a broken arm because of it.

The buzzer sounded and the gate opened and all thought stopped as the big animal lunged into the arena. The world was a blur, the roar of the crowd dim, as jolt after jolt shot through Wyatt. Yet he relished it and clung to the animal and let his anger and frustrations release in the battle between man and beast.

An eternity later the buzzer sounded. He heard the roar

of the crowd as cowboys tried to help him off the back of the bull.

He slid onto a horse and then dropped to the ground, running for the fence when the bull charged. He climbed the fence, perching on top to see the bull trot out through an open gate. His gaze swept the crowd and then returned to a box right on the front row.

Grace sat there watching him, and even across the big arena, he felt as if he was looking straight into her green eyes.

He dropped off the gate and crossed the empty space while they announced his time and everyone cheered. He was in the lead for the evening, but he barely heard anything. He didn't stop to think; he just kept walking, and when he reached her box, he jumped up, caught his hands on the wall and vaulted over to land on his feet. He sat down beside her. "What are you doing here?"

"I'm trying to change."

"It's a little late," he said.

She flinched as if he'd hit her. "It might be, but I decided you're right. I need to let go of some of my fears, and I thought the best way might be to come watch you ride. I love you, Wyatt."

He stared at her. "I've never been hurt like you hurt me."

"I'm sorry," she whispered, and closed her eyes.

"And I don't want to marry someone who wants me to change completely. I don't want to marry someone who feels sorry for me and is doing this out of charity."

"Charity!" Suddenly fire blazed in the depths of green. "Wyatt Sawyer, I would never marry a man out of charity. You're the last man on earth who needs a woman's charity. I love you! Just the way you are. Can't you understand that?" She threw her arms around his neck and kissed him, her soft lips on his, her tongue darting into his mouth as she pressed herself against him.

Wyatt was stunned momentarily, but then his arms wrapped around her and he kissed her back. He pulled her onto his lap, taking kisses that were salty with her tears. "Will you marry me?" he asked.

"Yes! Oh, yes. I love you!"

"Grace, you're going to drive me crazy." He kissed her again, and then he wanted to be alone with her. He wanted to make love to her, to peel away her clothes to make sure he wasn't dreaming. But there wasn't anything dreamlike about her kisses.

"I may lose Megan. You still want to marry me even if I don't have her?"

"Yes! And we're not going to lose her."

Some knot inside him loosened and fell away, and his world righted. "Let's get out of here." He stood and took her hand. People around them applauded and whistled, and he realized he'd forgotten where they were. He grinned, draped his arm across her shoulders and pulled her closer.

At his pickup, he hauled Grace into his arms to kiss her long and hard again. "Let's go home, darlin'. We have some making up and some celebrating to do."

Epilogue

Wyatt stood at the front of the sanctuary with Josh beside him as best man, Gabe next to Josh and Jett Colby as yet another groomsman. Grace's white-haired grandfather, Jeremy Talmadge, was officiating, and he smiled broadly, waiting for his granddaughter to appear.

Wyatt waited, watching Grace's sisters come down the aisle, followed by her good friend Virginia. Wyatt was barely aware of them or the crowded church. He glanced once at his soon-to-be mother-in-law, who held Megan in her arms. It was September now, only weeks since Grace had accepted his proposal, yet he felt as if he'd waited forever for this moment.

And then Grace appeared on the arm of her father, and Wyatt couldn't look anywhere else but at her. His heart thudded with joy.

Dressed in white, her thick, red hair pinned on top of her head, she looked lovelier than he'd ever seen her. He met her gaze, a gaze as direct as the day he'd first opened his door to meet her. Only now, her eyes were shining with love, and he felt a lump form in his throat. He loved her beyond measure, beyond anything he had ever dreamed. She had laid to rest so many skeletons of his past, helped him over hurts, solidified a place in the community for him. And won him Megan. Then Grace was beside him, her father placing her soft hand in his.

Wyatt drew a deep breath and squeezed her hand. He solemnly repeated vows with her, knowing he would love her forever.

Grace looked up at him as they were pronounced husband and wife, and then they hurried back down the long aisle. The day became a blur. First they had pictures taken at the church. Then they were driven to the country club for the reception, where more pictures were taken.

Wyatt had one taken with his groomsmen and then another with just Gabe and Josh, the three men looking happy, handsome, and still the closest of friends. Grace looked at Wyatt in his tux and white shirt. He was the handsomest man present, actually the best-looking Texan in the state, she thought, and she was still amazed how in love with her he was. Why had she thought she couldn't live with his wildness? That was part of what made him so exciting to her. Maybe she was indeed letting go of some of her conservative ways.

And he'd read the book she'd given him.

Next, Wyatt had another picture taken with his friends and their wives and children. Wyatt held Megan and Gabe held Ella, while Julian stood in front of them. The instant he was told he could go play again, Julian was off, rushing outside onto the large terrace where the other children were.

Later, the newlyweds were talking to their friends. "As

soon as you get back from your honeymoon,'' Gabe said, ''we'll have a barbecue and we'll all get together.''

''Sounds good to me,'' Wyatt replied.

''Then we'll have something at our place,'' Josh said, smiling at his wife as he hugged her thickening waist.

''When Megan gets a little bigger, she'll be able to play with Ella,'' Ashley said. ''I'm glad your custody battle is over, Wyatt.''

''Grace rescued me. I wondered at first if that's why she agreed to marry me,'' he said with a smile at his bride. He had his arm around her waist, and Grace was aware that any time he was near her, he held her hand or arm or put his arm around her—which suited her fine.

''But you knew better,'' she said, looking up into his dark eyes.

''As soon as I got engaged—especially to an upstanding, model citizen like Grace—the battle was over. They dropped the case. Their strongest point had been that I was a swinging bachelor. Grace ended that.''

While everyone laughed, Wyatt gave her a squeeze. ''I invited them to the wedding,'' he continued, ''because as I told them, I didn't want to cut them off from their granddaughter, but they declined to come.''

''Megan has other grandparents that love her,'' Josh remarked. ''I don't think your mother has put her down all day, except when she's been wanted for a photograph.''

''Mother's happy to have a granddaughter,'' Grace said, looking across the room at her mother and Megan.

''Our baby won't have grandparents,'' Laurie said, ''but I think our baby's aunts will be good substitutes.''

''I'm lucky to have my dad,'' Ashley remarked. ''He has Ella right now.''

"Well, Wyatt, that white stallion proves the old legend was true," Gabe said.

"Maybe so. Look at the three of us. His name is Legend now—really, Legend," Wyatt said grinning, and the others laughed. "It ought to be Maverick because he's a maverick," he said, looking down at Grace, and she remembered when Wyatt discovered she had ridden Legend. Wyatt had been angry and stunned, yet she thought maybe he had realized then that she had really begun to let go of her conservative ways.

In minutes other guests joined the group, and then Wyatt and Grace were separated. Once Wyatt was standing alone when his new father-in-law walked up.

Tom Talmadge smiled at Wyatt. "I want to thank you again for your more than generous donation to our mission work in Bolivia. It'll build a school and get us a small bus, among other things."

"My dad was tight and mean and never tried to help others," Wyatt said. "I like to think it's his money I'm giving. I guess I can't outgrow that feeling of wanting to get back at him. Something you'd never understand."

"I like to think it's your money, Wyatt. You're kind and generous beyond measure. You're a good person and you'll help children more than you can ever imagine."

"I was glad to do it. Would you two ever consider coming back here? There are kids in San Antonio who need help, too. I'd be happy to put up money, but I don't know anything about what to do."

Tom Talmadge glanced across the room. "I'll talk it over with Rose. We'll need to oversee your gift for the coming months, but once things get up and rolling, we might come back here. Megan is our first grandchild, and both of us want to get to know her."

"That would be great," Wyatt said, feeling a bond with Grace's father.

"Thanks for the offer. And don't worry about Megan while you're on your honeymoon."

"I'm not going to worry for a minute. She's in good hands. Thanks for keeping her and watching the ranch house while we're gone."

"It's been wonderful to get all the family together again. You've got a big family now, Wyatt."

"I'm glad. When I can find Grace, we'll be getting out of here, so I'll tell you goodbye now. You have all the phone numbers and hotels, and we'll call you tonight and every day."

The two men shook hands and Wyatt left. It was half an hour before he got Grace away from the party. They rushed out a back door to his waiting car, and he drove to his home in the city, where Grace changed into a green sheath dress and pumps and rushed back to the car.

In another half hour they were airborne, Wyatt piloting his jet as they headed to Houston. They would spend the night there and leave in the morning for ten days in Paris.

When they were finally alone in the bridal suite in Houston, Wyatt handed her a glass of champagne and raised his. "Here's to a lifetime of happiness, Mrs. Sawyer."

"I'll drink to that," Grace answered.

Both sipped their champagne, and then Wyatt took her glass from her and set it on the table beside his. He shed his coat and tie.

His dark eyes ablaze with love and desire, he slipped his arm around her waist and pulled her close. "Mrs. Sawyer. My wife. My love. Grace, I love you beyond words," he whispered.

She looped her arms around his neck and held him, standing on tiptoe and pulling his head down to kiss him.

Wyatt tightened his arms around her, his fingers caressing her nape and then pulling the back zipper of her dress slowly down. The material fell with a soft whisper around her ankles, but Grace was barely aware of it as she tried to unfasten the studs on Wyatt's shirt and unbuckle his belt. "Wyatt, I love you," she whispered.

He bent over her, and she clung to him while he kissed her deeply. Grace's heart thudded with excitement and joy as she held her reckless, handsome cowboy, the man she would cherish the rest of her life.

She leaned away to look up at him. "Now, wild man, let's see you really let go. I'm ready for a little excitement."

He grinned and his dark eyes glittered. "Always a challenge, Grace!" His arm tightened around her. "I'll see what I can do."

* * * * *

Silhouette®

Desire®

**Meet three sexy-as-all-get-out cowboys
in Sara Orwig's new Texas crossline miniseries**

STALLION PASS

These rugged bachelors may have given up on
love…but love hasn't given up on them!

Don't miss this steamy roundup of Texan tales!

DO YOU TAKE THIS ENEMY?
November 2002 (SD #1476)

ONE TOUGH COWBOY
December 2002 (IM #1192)

THE RANCHER, THE BABY & THE NANNY
January 2003 (SD #1486)

Available at your favorite retail outlet.

Silhouette®

Where love comes alive™

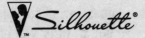

New York Times **Bestselling Author**

SUZANNE BROCKMANN

Blue McCoy was once the hero of Lucy Tait's teenaged dreams—quiet, dark and dangerous. After high school he left Hatboro Creek, South Carolina, to join the military.

Years later, now a navy SEAL, Blue is back in town, and Lucy is not the person he remembered. She's a no-nonsense police officer—and a woman Blue can't take his eyes off. But then Blue is accused of murder. And Lucy is assigned his case. Now their brief affair has become part of an extensive investigation, where what's at stake is critical— Blue's future...and maybe Lucy's heart.

FOREVER BLUE

"Thanks to Suzanne Brockmann's glorious pen, we all get to revel in heartstopping adventure and blistering romance."
—*Romantic Times*

MIRA®

Available the first week of February 2003 wherever paperbacks are sold!

Visit us at www.mirabooks.com

MSB680

COMING NEXT MONTH

#1489 SLEEPING BEAUTY'S BILLIONAIRE—Caroline Cross
Dynasties: The Barones
Years ago, Colleen Barone's mother had pressured her into breaking up with Gavin O'Sullivan. Then Colleen saw her gorgeous former flame at a wedding, and realized the old chemistry was still there. But the world-famous hotel magnate seemed to think she only wanted him now that he was rich. Somehow, Colleen had to convince Gavin she truly loved him—mind, body and soul!

#1490 KISS ME, COWBOY!—Maureen Child
After a bitter divorce, the last thing sexy single dad Mike Fallon wanted was to get romantically involved again. But when feisty Nora Bailey seemed determined to lose her virginity—with the town Casanova, no less—Mike rushed to her rescue. He soon found himself drowning in Nora's baby blues, but she wanted a husband. And he wasn't husband material…or was he?

#1491 THAT BLACKHAWK BRIDE—Barbara McCauley
Secrets!
Three days before her wedding, debutante Clair Beauchamp learned from handsome investigator Jacob Carver that she was really a Blackhawk from Texas. Realizing her whole life, including her almost-marriage, was a lie, Clair asked Jacob to reunite her with her family. But the impromptu road trip led to the consummation of their passionate attraction, and soon Clair yearned to make their partnership permanent.

#1492 CHARMING THE PRINCE—Laura Wright
Time was running out; if Prince Maxim Thorne didn't find a bride, his father would find one for him. So Max set out to seduce the lovely Francesca Charming, certain his father would never agree to his marrying a commoner and would thus drop his marriage demand. But what started out as make-believe turned into undeniable passion…. Might marrying Francesca give Max the fairy-tale ending he hadn't known he wanted?

#1493 PLAIN JANE & THE HOTSHOT—Megan McKinney
Matched in Montana
Shy Joanna Lofton met charismatic smoke-jumping firefighter Nick Kramer while on a mountain retreat. Joanna worried she wasn't exciting enough for a man like Nick, but her fears proved unfounded, for the fires raging around them couldn't compare to the flame of attraction burning between them.

#1494 AT THE TYCOON'S COMMAND—Shawna Delacorte
When Kim Donaldson inherited a debt to Jared Stevens's family, she agreed to work as Jared's assistant for the summer. Despite a generations-old family feud, as Kim and Jared worked together, their relationship took a decidedly romantic turn. But could they put the past behind them before it tore them apart?